WHAT OTHERS ARE SAYING

Three Wars is a compelling and inspirational finale to *The Kansas NCO* trilogy. A prequel, the families of the beloved characters from the first two books struggle through war and peace, culminating when the young characters from *The Kansas NCO* and *Back To The World* depart for their harrowing tours of duty in Vietnam. I strongly recommend Three Wars, a heartfelt story of three families who prevail through war and triumph in peace.

~ *Maria Theresa T. Booth, Special Education Teacher*

Much has been written about WWII, Korea, and Vietnam, and authors typically focus on the differences between the three wars. Joe Campolo Jr, in his new book, *Three Wars*, pinpoints the commonality of war and relationships. He understands that although battlefields exist in diverse settings, humans respond similarly. He writes with an authenticity that is critical in historical fiction. His insight into the human psyche and perception of the ties between generations make him an extraordinary storyteller.

~ *Pat McGrath-Avery, Author*

"*Three Wars* is a perfect prequel to *The Kansas NCO* trilogy, bringing the story together and on to its conclusion. It truly was inspiring to see how the three families became heroes and warriors, doing their best to bring peace during times of war. It has been quite the journey to see the characters grow and develop throughout the trilogy and how the stories and families intertwine and inspire. Like *The Kansas NCO* and *Back to The World*, *Three Wars* was impossible to put down, opening up superbly by leading into the very first book where the journey started. *Three Wars'* finale is powerful and upbeat, leaving the promise of hope for the future."

~ *Adam Honey*

THREE WARS

JOE CAMPOLO JR.

Library of Congress Control Number: 2018942959

ISBN: 978-1-943267-53-8 Trade paperback

ISBN: 978-1-943267-54-5 Ebook

Cover Design by Sandi Linhart

Edited by Betsy Beard

Printed in the United States.

This book is dedicated to

My father, Joseph F. Campolo Sr., World War II
U.S. Army, 32nd Cavalry Reconnaissance Squadron
Ardennes Counteroffensive, Battle of the Bulge
Deceased 1978

My uncle, John Campolo, World War II
U.S. Army, 109th Infantry Regiment
Battle of the Bulge
Killed in Action—September 15, 1944

My father-in-law, William R. Kuessow, World War II
U.S. Army, 10th Mountain Division
Italian Campaign
Deceased 2006

My friend, Frank Romero, Korean War
U.S. Army, 8th Army Headquarters

My friend, Richard Williams, Veteran
U.S. Air Force, 18th Fighter Interceptor Squadron
Deceased 2018

The Crucianellis

Dante Crucianelli: Born in 1922, one of fourteen children born to an impoverished Italian American family from Southeastern Wisconsin. Enlisted in the U.S. Army in 1941 and trained as a paratrooper. Older brother of Mario and uncle of Andrew Crucianelli. Dante served in World War II, European Theater.

Mario Crucianelli: Born in 1928, younger brother of Dante Crucianelli. Enlisted in the U.S. Army in 1948. Father of Andrew Crucianelli. Mario served in the Korean War.

Andrew Crucianelli: Born in 1949, the son of Mario and Delia Crucianelli. Nephew of Dante Crucianelli. Enlisted in the U.S. Air Force in 1968 and volunteered for Vietnam. Nicknamed Cru. Andrew served in the Vietnam War.

The Redmonds

Ishkode Redmond: Born in 1922, a Native American of the Ojibwa tribe, and raised on the White Earth Indian Reservation in Northern Minnesota. Enlisted in the U.S. Marine Corps in 1941. Older brother of Chibenashi Redmond and uncle of Arnold Redmond. Ishkode served in World War II, Pacific Theater.

Chibenashi Redmond: Born in 1925, the younger brother of Ishkode Redmond and father of Arnold Redmond. Enlisted in U.S. Marines when Korean War broke out. Nicknamed Bird. Chibenashi served in the Korean War.

Arnold Redmond: Born in 1948, the son of Chibe-nashi and Morning Star Redmond. Nephew of Ishkode Redmond. Enlisted in U.S. Marines in 1966 and transferred to Air Force. Nicknamed Red or Chief. Arnold served in the Vietnam War.

The Montrells

Raymond Montrell: Born in 1919 and started as a crop duster in rural Ohio while in high school. Interrupted college at Ohio State and went to Canada to help in the World War II effort before U.S. involvement. Father of Douglas Montrell. Raymond served in World War II and the Korean War.

Douglas Montrell: Born in 1949, the son of Raymond and Marion Montrell. Enlisted in the U.S. Air Force after high school and deployed to Vietnam in the fall of 1969. Doug served in the Vietnam War.

PROLOGUE

"**D**amn, that was close!"

The strong smell of cordite drifted through the air, mixing with the damp jungle odor. Andrew Crucianelli, Arnold Redmond, and Doug Montrell sat in a hide they had found for the night, while the Vietcong attempted to flush them out.

Thirty minutes passed without further mortar fire.

"Think maybe they gave up, now that it's dark," Montrell whispered.

"Seems like it. Guess we better get some sleep," Redmond said. "I'll take first watch."

Crucianelli was lying on a sleeping pallet made with brush. "I suppose Red would shoot me if I lit up a cigarette."

Montrell laughed. "I'll shoot you, too, if you've been hoarding all the damn smokes."

"Hell, Cru smokes 'em right down to the filter, and then saves the filter to burn when he's all out of stubs." Redmond lifted his weapons and peered into the darkness. "Ya know, Cru, those damn things will probably kill you before the VC do."

"Monty and I need extra vices to compensate for you, since you're the holiest goddamn Injun in the whole world."

After a short silence, Cru said. "What I wouldn't give to be back at Phu Cat, sucking down a nice cup of coffee. Guess my old man would appreciate this shit detail, out in the middle of nowhere. He never smoked, but he always mentioned how good a hot cup of joe tasted when he was an Army grunt in Korea. Like it was somehow special...or tasted better than the coffee Mom made."

"Your dad was in Korea?"

"Yep. Private First Class Mario Crucianelli."

Montrell smiled. "My old man served in Korea, too. Air Force, though—pilot with the 98th Bombardment Wing. He used to say the same thing about the coffee. He told me those B-29s were cold as ice boxes, and the only thing that kept 'em warm was a thermos of coffee and enemy fire."

"Small world." Cru stretched as much as he could in the cramped hide. "My dad was at Pusan. Got into some trouble there, so I guess he'd know how we feel right about now."

"My dad was a Marine. He was in Pusan, too, I think," Red said quietly.

That surprised Cru. "What? I've never heard you talk about your dad at all,"

"Yeah, well that's cause there's not much to tell," Red ducked his head. "My Uncle Ishkode served in World War Two. He used to tell me the coffee was cold and weak... just like our Indian agent on the White Earth res. He'd say given a choice, he always drank the beer the Saipan natives brewed. Strong stuff."

Montrell peered at Red through the darkness. He sensed Red was uneasy but was trying to conceal it. "Saipan, huh? Guess my dad's older than both of your dads. He was in the big one and the Korean War. He flew bombing missions out of Saipan at some point. But he had to wait until the Marines cleared the island. He must have gotten there after your uncle did all the dirty work, Red. Small world..."

Red had enough of the conversation. "Yeah, well, you two keep jawing and pretty soon first watch will be over, unless the gooks hear us first. Like I said before, better get some sleep."

The three drifted off into their own thoughts, remembering fathers and uncles who had fought in their own wars before them, experiencing their own hardships and grief.

And each one of them, living or dead, had a story to tell.

PART ONE

*Through our parents we look behind us, through our
children we look ahead.*

WORLD WAR TWO

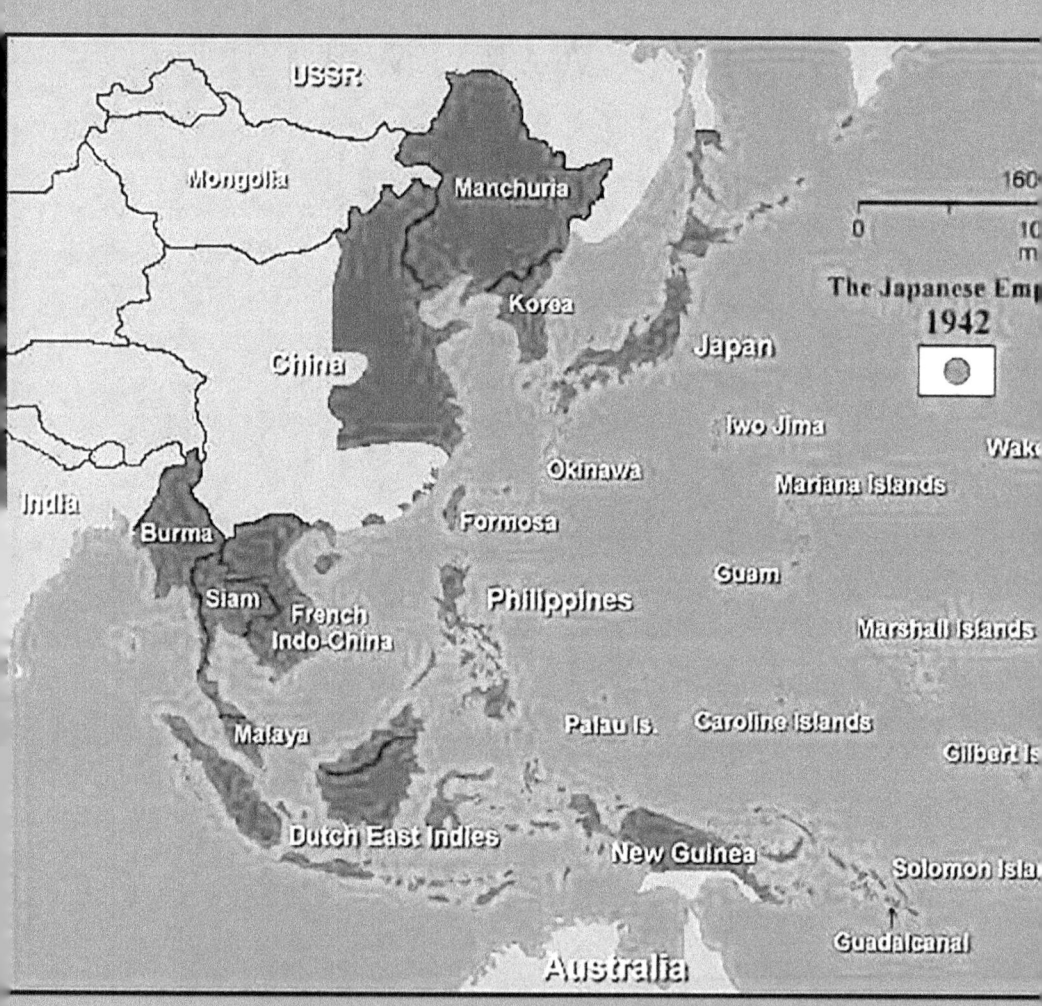

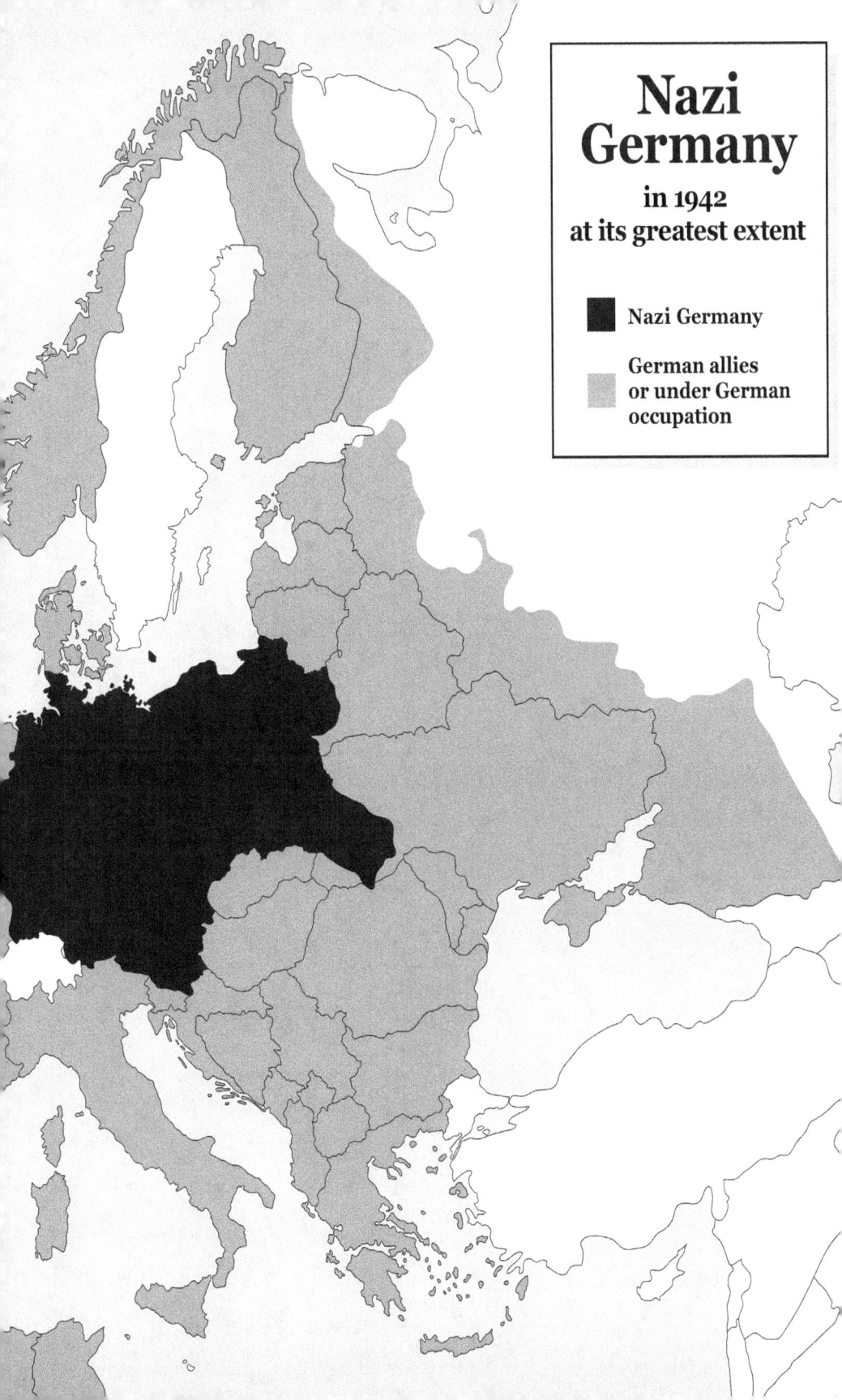

Nazi Germany

in 1942
at its greatest extent

Nazi Germany

German allies
or under German
occupation

CHAPTER 1

JUNE 1944

NORMANDY, FRANCE

U.S. ARMY 82ND AIRBORNE DIVISION

Private First Class Dante Crucianelli looked at the men, packed tight against the sides of the C-47. The ride was noisy, cold, and bumpy. The weather had not cooperated, and the gusting wind made this the worst jump they had ever made. Everyone looked sick as the plane bucked and juked.

Dante leaned over and shouted into Corporal Donald Hester's helmet. "Well, the ride hasn't cheered up old hard-ass yet. Maybe when they open the door, the wind will blow all the ugly off that mug of his."

"That'd be okay with me," Hester yelled, a faint smile coming to his lips.

The object of their conversation, Private Virgil Shields, sat directly across from them, glowering. Shields was a chronically ill-tempered member of the platoon, but Dante begrudgingly admired him. Although a cantankerous son of a bitch, Shields was made for this kind of shit. He had ice water in his veins.

Hester, Crucianelli, Shields, and the other fifteen men on the aircraft were among the 13,000 paratroopers of the United States Army currently in the air or soon to be. Elements of the 82nd and the 101st Airborne Divisions were flying into Normandy from the west, ready to be dropped

1

behind enemy lines. They'd boarded the C-47 just after midnight, hoping the darkness and the element of surprise would mitigate the fact that they would be sitting ducks in a shooting gallery if the Germans looked up.

Once they were on the ground and reunited with each other and their equipment, the paratroopers would be tasked with securing bridges, eliminating pockets of resistance, and preventing German reinforcements from entering the peninsula. Their orders were to destroy anything that could impede the main Allied force that would be landing on the beaches of Normandy at dawn.

To avoid German shooters as well as high winds, the paratroopers had to jump at low altitude. This, of course, presented a problem if the chutes didn't open rapidly, resulting in possible high casualties when men hit the ground too quickly. But it was a trade-off—stealth for casualties.

As the aircraft reached the drop zone, the load master alerted Command Sergeant Lamar Motzfield. A bright red light flashed and a crackling buzzer sounded, increasing the tension among the men. On Motzfield's signal, the paratroopers struggled to their feet, more than fifty pounds of equipment strapped to their backs and filling their pockets. They turned to face the rear door, preparing themselves to leave the relative safety of the plane.

Dante yelled over his shoulder to Hester. "Here we go, buddy. It's fuck time."

Standing at the exit door, Motzfield shouted down the chatting among the nervous troops. "Shut up, sky soldiers! Grab your strap and concentrate on your jump. The wind hasn't died down, so remember what you were told about getting separated. Good luck, airborne troopers. See you back in the dirt."

The men shuffled toward the door. "Go!"

"Go!"

"Go!" Motzfield gave each man a push as they left the aircraft.

Fortunately, the wind did not blow them over squads of German shooters as other flights were experiencing. They did, however, have to deal with the uneven surface of farm fields and sparsely wooded valleys and draws. The ground came up fast because of the low altitude jump, and paratroopers were injured as they plopped hard on the rough terrain. The medics who dropped among them had only to listen for the screams and moans to find their next casualty.

Dante landed hard. His feet shot forward and he landed on his ass. Dropping his rifle, he fumbled for the release, while gathering his chute.

Hester jerked to a stop, his chute caught on a low branch. He could see the ground two feet below, so he released and dropped gently to the edge of the field.

Shields landed with a thud next to a small group of trees.

Though banged up, none of the three were injured. They collected themselves and looked for the source of the screaming that was rending the air nonstop. Two of the men from their flight had landed in the trees. One was impaled by a branch—from his groin all the way up through his neck. Though dead on impact, the look of horror on the man's face would be frozen in time, forever etched in the memory of those who witnessed it.

The screaming came from the other man, who was caught by a smaller branch that penetrated his upper arm and exited near his collar bone. His chute and lines were tangled in the tree. The man was alive but in terrible pain.

Watching the poor man, Hester grimaced. "I'll go up and get him."

Crucianelli watched as the nimble Hester scrambled up the tree.

Shields, who seldom missed an opportunity to mess with Dante, sniffed loudly, then sniffed again. "You know, you really stink, Crucianelli. More than usual."

"What the hell?"

"I mean, you really do smell bad. Did you shit yourself?" Shields bent over laughing.

"Hardly. I think I would know," Dante examined his rifle and then peered down at his boots. The moon gave enough light that he could see clumps of dark matter clinging to his soles. "It's shit, all right! Fresh cow pie. Must've landed in a nice big fat pile of it. Want some?" He scraped at his boots with a dead branch.

"Heads up," Hester called down. He'd cut the impaling branch from the tree with his survival knife and was lowering the moaning paratrooper—branch and all—to Shields and Crucianelli. The man started screaming again.

"Where're all these goddamn medics?" Shields was impatient for someone to come and shut the bastard up.

By the time Hester climbed back down, a medic had already arrived and taken over.

"We better get our gear and get to the regroup area," Hester said. "If anyone spots Motzfield, yell."

Dante could see dark forms around them, small groups of men collecting themselves and their gear, then moving off. Getting lost would not be a problem, at least. Much to his relief, he heard no shooting, indicating they hadn't landed in the middle of a German defensive position.

Dante was alarmed by the screaming and moaning. "Sure hope we haven't taken too many casualties already, maybe we should look for more injured guys and try to help."

Shields had to inject his opinion on that. "Better let the officers do the thinking, Crucianelli, if they need any fruit picked, they can just ask. Of course, if you try to help the wounded, they'll probably die, just from the smell."

Having had several dust-ups with Shields, Dante wasn't going to take that standing still. He threw down his backpack and rifle, and squared off at Shields, who did the same.

Corporal Hester wasn't having any of it. "Knock it off,

you two. We got a war to fight here. You know…with the Germans. Stow it or I'll put you on report first chance I get."

Dante backed off. He picked up his gear and took off, not waiting for Hester and Shields.

"Fucker's deserting." Shields scowled.

Hester got in Shields' face. "I'm gonna tell you something. And I'm only gonna say it once. I don't like you, and I don't know anyone that does. You keep fucking with people and I'll give you every shit detail from here to Berlin." He pushed Shields forward. "Now shut up and get your ass moving."

Shields and Crucianelli remained silent as they trudged through the rough farm fields and draws along with the other men who survived the jump. Although there were still isolated pockets of injured men, most of the casualties had been tended to and were being sent to a small field hospital that had been hastily set up.

"Looks like the regroup area," Hester noted as they came upon an encampment of tents brimming with officers and radio operators. They found their officer in charge, Captain Charles Drummond.

As more and more men straggled in, Drummond greeted each of them. "Good to see you three. Sergeant Motzfield and the rest of your platoon are setting up on the east side." He waved his arm in the general direction. "Get your gear over there. The gliders are coming in with our jeeps and the rest of our equipment. Motzfield will brief you."

Hester saluted the captain. "Thank you, sir. We'll find him."

Sergeant Motzfield and about three quarters of the platoon worked feverishly to set up camp. The three reported to the sergeant for orders.

"Yeah, this is what's left after the jump." Motzfield saw their forlorn looks. "Set up your tents and get some chow. After that we'll go over tomorrow's doings—well, today actually—and set up our watch schedule. You three can catch some sleep first."

After eating their K-rations and attending their first combat briefing, they settled in for a brief rest. Hester and Crucianelli bunked together, as usual, while Shields bunked with one of the few men in the platoon who could tolerate him.

They had a full day ahead. Their war was just beginning.

***

It was a week later. Drenched in sweat, PFC Crucianelli blew out the deep breath he had been holding for what seemed like an eternity. Members of the rifle squad gathered around the jeep, slapping his back and beating on his helmet.

"Hot damn, Dante. You did it!"

As a designated driver, Dante made good use of the training he had obtained while garrisoned in England for two months prior to the D-Day invasion. He'd acquired his driving skills, however, much earlier.

Raised in a small Wisconsin city, Dante delivered vegetables for his uncle, Silvio Crucianelli. Uncle Silvio demanded that all vegetable deliveries be made prior to the start of Dante's school day at eight o'clock in the morning. Dodging traffic, bad roads, and revenue-hungry law enforcement officers, Dante's shrewd driving ensured that Uncle Silvio and his customers were kept happy.

Along with the other designated drivers from the 82nd Airborne, Dante had spent countless hours going over the maps in the area of Normandy where they would be dropped. It was their task to identify and nullify German positions inland, so as to smooth the way for the bulk of the invading force moving in from Omaha Beach. Dante and the other drivers were able to maneuver around the telltale humps and markings where mines had been planted in the roads of the once delightful area of Northern France.

But a bigger threat turned out to be snipers.

Outfitted with Mauser Kar 98K bolt-action rifles with scopes, German snipers had been picking off drivers since they'd left the drop area. So far, seven drivers had been killed—along with several passengers—as a result of vehicular crashes. After getting pinned down by snipers, the officer in charge of the convoy typically sent a rifle squad to search and destroy each nest. That could take up to half a day, which riled upper command, so P-51 Mustang fighter bombers from England were to take out the sniper.

The German sniper's general location would be determined and the information communicated to the P-51, which would drop several bombs on the suspected location. It was a good method for taking out both the sniper and his spotter. And the tactic worked well enough to allow the convoy to move on. The trick was to get the sniper to fire when the P-51 was in the area, so the ground troops could determine his general location.

Volunteer drivers played a deadly game of chicken to present a ripe target. Tempted with such easy pickings, the snipers would fire away. If the "chicken" from the 82nd was fast—and lucky, the sniper would miss. So far, Dante Crucianelli had been fast and lucky.

Proceeding to their assigned checkpoint, the men set-up a perimeter and dug in. Further orders would be arriving soon, assigning areas of operation where the platoons would recon and take out German defensive positions within their capability. Larger defensive bunkers were to be identified so they could be targeted by air and naval weapons.

***

Within a few weeks, the beaches of Normandy were secured and Allied troops were moving inland. The ever-clever Germans continued to foil the plans of the 82nd Airborne's advance units, employing mobile hit-and-run teams that would decimate approaching troops and then move on to wreak havoc on other advancing infantry troops.

Hester and Crucianelli now lay in a cold water-filled depression. Other members of the platoon were in similar depressions and gullies scattered around the bottom of the barren hill. A concealed machine-gun nest had opened up on them as they reached the mid-point of their climb.

"What the hell are we gonna do, Danny?" Hester screamed.

Heavy caliber bullets flew just inches over his and Dante's position, shredding vegetation as the two clung to the bottom of the depression.

"I think half our guys are dead up there," Crucianelli yelled over the din. "We're gonna have to fall back."

Hester didn't dare move. "How the fuck we gonna fall back? We move a goddamn inch, we'll get blown away."

"We'll time their reloading pattern. They have to stop and reload. And we'll make a run for it when they do."

After ten minutes Crucianelli had calculated the reloading pattern, and when the next reload was due, he screamed, "Run!"

The two jumped up and dashed thirty yards back, taking cover behind a large tree stump. Other members of the platoon, taking their cue, got up and scrambled back as well. Not all found cover in time. As the German gun came back to life, it mowed down two more members of the platoon. Farther back and in better cover, the rest were still pinned down by the German gun.

"At least we can shoot back now," Hester yelled.

Isolated pockets of men began to return fire, and the pace of the heavy German gun slowed down. Crucianelli and Hester were taking aim when Sergeant Motzfield jumped alongside of them, nearly knocking them out into the open.

The large man barked out an order. "Fix bayonets!"

"What's the deal, Sarge?" Hester asked.

"Gonzales is up in a tree. He's gonna plink at that Kraut nest until we can sneak up on 'em. He's already started. With their position at the top of the hill, we won't be able to shoot them, but once we're up there we can jump into their nest and finish them off with bayonets. Everyone's on board and ready when you are."

Dante and Hester fixed bayonets on their M1 Garand rifles. "Ready, Sarge."

Motzfield held up his arm, and at his signal every remaining man from 2nd Platoon rushed up the hill. The heavy gun, occupied in trying to shoot Gonzales out of his tree, now came down to fire on the attackers running up the hill.

Before it could train on the incoming men, several reached the top and jumped into the nest. More followed, all of them savagely bayoneting the five Germans in the nest until Motzfield gave the order to stop.

"Gonzales, stop firing and get down!" Motzfield yelled, although Gonzales had stopped shooting when the first GI crested the hill and jumped into the nest.

In the sudden silence, the remaining men of 2nd Platoon took a short rest to steady their nerves. When Motzfield gave the order, they collected their dead and wounded and headed back to camp.

Days later, disaster struck again when they stumbled upon another German machine gun nest. When the GIs were within thirty feet of the emplacement, the Germans commenced firing

Five men were immediately shredded by the large caliber rounds. Of the five, three died instantly. Dante crawled toward one of the remaining two.

"Keep breathing, man, keep breathing." Dante attempted to put a compress on his comrade's chest wound, but the man's last gasp whooshed out of his chest like a bicycle tire with a spike through it.

Corporal Hester crouched nearby, staring at the dead

men. His voice shook. "The Sarge is dead. What the fuck are we gonna do?"

"We'll be okay, Hester. We can't panic," Dante said. "You're in charge now, buddy. Let's try to remember our training. We need to fall back and regroup...and we're gonna take out that fucking machine gun," he added with conviction.

Hester shook his head a couple of times. "Yeah, okay, Danny. Can you call the other men back?"

Dante gathered up the remaining squad members and laid out a plan.

"The Krauts don't have three-hundred-sixty-degree capability with that heavy gun. Some of you are gonna get their attention, while three of us work our way around back. We'll attack them from behind, toss in a couple pine-apples. Any questions?"

Still in shock from the initial attack, Hester didn't yet have his wits about him. The other members of the squad looked at Hester, trying to determine if he was in any kind of shape to validate Dante's plan.

Hester recovered a bit, "Sounds good, Danny. Where do you want us?"

"You hang back. When I give you the high sign, unleash everything you've got on that nest."

Dante pointed to two of the remaining men, saying, "You're with me."

The three eased back, slowly working their way around the machine gun nest until they were directly behind it. Dante's head swiveled constantly, alert for any other Germans that might be in the vicinity. Within fifteen minutes, the three had aligned themselves thirty yards behind the nest. They belly-crawled to within fifteen yards, stopping every minute or so to listen. Once set, Dante threw a large rock over the nest toward Hester and the rest of the squad. "Stay low so we don't get hit by our own men," Dante reminded the two with him.

"That's the signal!" Hester yelled. "Open fire with everything you've got."

Dante motioned his two men forward. When they were ten yards from the nest, they pulled the pins on their grenades and waited several seconds before tossing them in.

The grenades were Mk III concussion grenades, designed to kill the occupants of rooms and bunkers by means of a stunning blast. The grenades expelled a certain amount of shrapnel, but the bodies and equipment would not be shredded as severely as they would be with a fragmentation grenade.

In their first briefing back in camp, Captain Drummond emphasized the importance of gathering intelligence from the German troops they encountered.

"The Allies need to know if the Germans we're facing are occupation forces or special Nazi forces sent in to impede the invasion," Drummond had told his men. "The intelligence we glean could save countless lives. We need unit designations, maps, correspondence, and even letters from sweethearts. Whenever you succeed in killing these bastards, make sure you gather everything you can. And get it back to us ASAP."

Dante and his squad members confirmed that the Germans were dead and the machine gun was destroyed in the blast. They extracted personal effects and paperwork from the nest.

Then they picked up their dead comrades and headed back to operational headquarters.

***

"Looks like you've got yourself a rifle squad, Crucianelli."

"Yes, sir. Will you inform the men?"

"That's your first order." Captain Drummond looked up from the after-action report. Seeing Crucianelli squirm, he asked, "Problem?"

"Well, sir...it's just that having a PFC running a squad might rub a few of the boys the wrong way."

"Good point." Captain Drummond took a set of chevrons out of his pocket and tossed them to Dante. "Problem solved, Sergeant Crucianelli."

Dante picked up the chevron patches and stared at them. "Thank you, Captain. I'll do the best job I can."

Drummond was blunt. "If you don't, it'll be the last job you do." Then he struck a more conciliatory tone. "Don't fret, Dante. Just use your instinct and follow your training. You have my confidence. Now go inform your men."

Dante went to his squad area. He felt he should tell Hester first so he wouldn't feel snookered. Hester took the news in stride.

"I'm happy for you, Danny. I'll back you any way I can, but you're gonna have to deal with Shields."

Dante frowned. "Yeah, Shields ain't gonna like this one bit. But until Ike gives him a couple stripes, he'll have to deal with it."

Dante didn't have to wait long to deal with Shields. Within ten minutes, the rest of the rifle squad showed up at Dante's tent, led by a red-faced Shields.

Shields, the son of a wheat farmer from Nebraska, had been on Dante's ass ever since the two met. When he wasn't calling Dante a dago or a wop, he was calling him a fascist fink. Shields wasn't entirely responsible for the bad blood, as Dante would refer to Shields on occasion as plowboy or Alfalfa. The two had come to blows on more than one occasion, having to be separated by other members of the rifle squad.

"So the fascists are running the Army now," Shields fumed.

Dante ignored the insult and addressed the group.

"Captain Drummond has made me the squad leader. He also promoted me to sergeant, though I haven't had a chance to sew the stripes on yet."

This information riled Shields to a new level. "So it's Sergeant Dago, is it? I don't have to salute you, do I?"

Enraged, Dante grabbed Shields by the collar and threw him to the ground. "Now listen, you fucking bunk lizard. I'm the squad leader now and I outrank you. Keep fucking with me, I'll give you every shit detail that comes up. You want to duke it out? Get up and we'll do it, but win or lose, I ain't taking any more of your shit."

The other men in the squad backed up.

"Knock his block off, Sarge," a squad member yelled. "Don't eat any shit from that hog head, Dante," came from another.

No comments were made on Shields behalf.

Taken aback by Crucianelli's ferocity and the obvious support Dante had from the other men, Shields remained on the ground—red with rage, but idle.

After making eye contact with each man, Dante spoke, "We're going out again tomorrow. Three new replacements will be with us. I expect everyone to bring them up to speed, because we won't have time to do any training in camp."

Dante glared at Shields. "Get up. I expect all members of the squad to perform their duties as ordered. Any concerns, questions, or issues: talk to me."

CHAPTER 2

Private First Class Ishkode Redmond, a sniper with the 2nd Marine Division, inched away from the position he'd held for almost an hour. After he situated himself, he locked onto his target with his scope. His spotter, PFC Harold Karsten, repositioned himself accordingly. Ishkode waited in thick canopy forty feet in the air and approximately seven-hundred yards from the entrance of a cave. He was tasked on this mission with killing Colonel Hoshi Nakahara, the Japanese commanding officer responsible for the defense of half the island of Saipan. Ishkode and his spotter had been in their hide for two days, waiting for the colonel to present himself.

During the long wait, Ishkode's mind drifted back to his youth, growing up on the Ojibwa reservation in Northern Minnesota. Life on the res was often harsh and unfulfilling for the Native Americans who had been warehoused there. The government discouraged the Ojibwa from practicing their native culture, attempting to supplant it with the white man's Christian beliefs. Ishkode's family, like all the others at White Earth Indian Reservation, resented the attempt to convert them from their spiritual roots.

Ishkode had many positive—as well as negative—memories from those days. But it was the one that had gotten him here that occupied his mind now. In an attempt to appease the Bureau of Indian Affairs, tribal leaders had sent him—along with his brothers and sisters—to the local "white man's" school. Uncomfortable and unwelcome, Ishkode was often truant and frequently in trouble.

As a teen, Ishkode and several other young members of the tribe worked for the Indian agency on the reservation, performing a variety of manual labor tasks on an as-needed basis. When the Depression hit, the Ojibwa, like many Native Americans, took no notice of it. The quality of their life was no better or worse than it had been before the economic disaster occurred. The Ojibwa kept up their traditional practices of trapping, hunting, fishing, and gathering from the forests and fields to fill their larders. Surplus money the Indians earned from their trapping furs was sent to a central bank through their local Indian Agent. During this time, Ishkode's mother was a clerk in the Indian Agent's office and took care of the routine paperwork and minor bookkeeping duties. She discovered that the Indian Agent was siphoning money from the White Earth trapping accounts and funneling the funds to his personal account in the same bank. When she confronted the man, he threatened to frame her for the embezzling.

Ishkode found out about the incident some months after his seventeenth birthday and beat the Indian Agent severely. With the tribal police after him, Ishkode left school without notice, gathered his gear at home, and fled to the far side of the reservation. He camped out for three weeks, living off the land. But fearing that the agent would retaliate against his mother, Ishkode turned himself in to tribal police. By then, the agent's financial misappropriations had been discovered. He was terminated from his position and was sent up against charges. Unfortunately, Ishkode was also charged—for assault.

During Ishkode's trial, the local protestant minister, a good man despite his cultural arrogance, came to Ishkode's defense. He told of how Ishkode helped anyone in need and always made sure the Indian children at the white man's school were treated fairly. The judge allowed Ishkode to enlist in the military rather than face a jail sentence. Given the choice between another trip to juvenile jail or a bunk with the United States military, he had chosen to enlist.

Now in Saipan in a hide with Harold, Ishkode sensed the time might be near for his target to reveal himself.

Several low-ranking officers and enlisted men had walked in and out of the cave several times, furtively scanning the area.

Harold gave a thumbs-up and both men tensed. A small man with no rank or insignia on his uniform walked out of the cave, surrounded by several larger men.

"The bastard's hiding behind that fucking sumo wrestler," Harold whispered. "You may have to take a chance and shoot through him.

Ishkode gave the okay sign and palmed the bolt of his M1903 Springfield. Although some U.S. military snipers had gone to newer weapons as the war moved into 1944, Ishkode still preferred his weathered old Springfield. He liked the weight and balance and had taken out more than a few Japanese with the rifle. Looking through his scope, Ishkode held his breath and squeezed off three shots in short succession. He turned to Harold, who was observing through his spotting scope.

The large man in front of Colonel Nakahara crumpled to the ground. Harold signaled thumbs up. A split second later, Nakahara stumbled and fell. A red stain blossomed where he was hit dead center in the chest with the second round from the .30-06 caliber rifle. Efficient as always, Ishkode hit a lower grade officer standing to the left of Nakahara with his third shot. The bullet caught the man in the throat, and he died with a look of anger on his face.

As armed Japanese soldiers poured out of the cave, Ishkode and Harold moved into their egress procedure, folding up their gear and stashing it in rucksacks. Using their predetermined escape route, they moved away rapidly. The predictable return fire from the Japs blasted trees and vegetation all around them. Hunched over, they hustled to get out of range of machine-gun fire, which was due to erupt at any moment—usually a minute or two after the initial barrage of small arms fire.

Ishkode and Harold heard the rat-a-tat staccato from a heavy machine gun just as they rounded a hill large enough to shield them from any further shooting from the cave.

Ishkode held up for a second. "They'll be sending out patrols in a minute or two. Which way do you want to go?"

"I'll take the B route," Harold said. "Safe travels. See you at camp."

The men split up according to procedure. If an armed patrol caught up with one man, chances were good that he could keep the Japanese distracted long enough for the other man to make his escape. Skilled snipers and spotters were highly valued. U.S. Marine Corps protocol required sniper teams to do whatever they could to return and fight another day—even if it meant abandoning their partner. Ishkode and Harold knew the drill and followed it as ordered. With any luck, they'd both arrive back at the American camp in the next few hours.

***

Back at the operational camp Ishkode reported the details of the successful mission to his OIC, Captain Richard Andersen, and then waited at the perimeter for Harold to show up. It had been two hours already.

Ishkode and Harold had been among the 18,000 Marines who fought through Tarawa in November of 1943. Casualties had been high—more than 1,000 killed and well over 2,000 wounded. The Marines made the Japanese pay dearly, however, killing 4,500 in the deadly battle that lasted a mere seventy-six hours.

The snipers were tasked with taking out the Japanese officer corps. However, the action had moved so quickly that Harold and Ishkode had hardly set up a hide before the entire Marine division was upon them. Both Ishkode and Harold had been wounded in the heavy fighting in Tarawa, neither one seriously. Hobbled with a leg wound, Ishkode was carried back to safety by Harold, who had to stop every fifty feet or so to wipe the blood out of his eyes from his own scalp wound.

After recovering from their wounds, the two took part in several small skirmishes with the island-hopping U.S. forces. Then in February of 1944 they fought in the Battle of Eniwetok with the 22nd U.S. Marine Regiment. Though not as intense as Tarawa, Eniwetok presented a unique problem for the two snipers. There, the Japanese used spider holes to slow the Marines' advance. They would pop out of their tiny holes in the ground, shoot Marines, and then slip back into their concealed hides. Ishkode and Harold's job was to sit in their nest and wait. Once a Jap popped out of his hide, he fell under the deadly eye of the skilled sniping team of Harold and Ishkode. Evidence of their success was the number of dead Japanese soldiers lying half in and half out of spider holes all over Eniwetok. Neither Harold nor Ishkode was injured, and they were able to take part in the Saipan campaign from its inception.

Over their months together, they grew as close as brothers. They could recite each other's family members, hometowns, life histories, and even immunization records. They depended on each other for life—literally.

While Ishkode waited, he thought about Harold's family back home. Harold was one of those guys who got mail—a lot of mail. And pictures. Wherever they bunked, be it a tent, bunker, or out in the boonies somewhere, Harold always managed to find a place to hang pictures.

"You must have thirty sisters," Ishkode teased.

"Yeah, and half of them are in love with you." Through

letters and photos, Harold's family knew Ishkode almost as well as they knew Harold. "If you don't come back to Pennsylvania with me, they probably won't let me back in the house."

"No sign of him?"

Ishkode was startled back into the present by Captain Andersen's question.

"No." Ishkode shook his head. "Can I go after him, sir?"

The captain pursed his lips. "You know the deal, Ishkode. We'll do whatever we can in God's name to get Harold back, but you can't go."

Marines were not in the habit of leaving members behind, and the 2nd Marine Division most definitely adhered to that practice. Ishkode and his spotter were rare commodities, and the Marines couldn't afford to lose one of them, let alone two. An infantry team would be sent out and they would expend every effort to find Lance Corporal Harold Karsten.

Ishkode continued to pace back and forth along the perimeter long after the captain left. He tried to anticipate where Harold would enter the compound if he found his way back.

Damn! Captain should have let me go after him. As time crawled by, Ishkode knew deep down that Harold would not return. He wondered how the family would react. He envisioned the telegram that would deliver the dreaded news. He imagined one of the sisters running and hiding at the sight of the Western Union man. Ishkode spoke out loud, almost shouting. "C'mon, buddy! We promised we'd get through this shit together. And I'm holding you to it." He continued to walk the perimeter, thinking maybe he could scold Harold into showing up.

But deep down Ishkode knew. He knew.

***

Two days later, Captain Andersen called Ishkode to his tent.

"You need to hook up with another spotter, Ishkode, we can't wait for Harold any longer. Headquarters has another big fish they need taken out. And we all know it's Ishkode Redmond that takes out the biggest fish."

Ishkode's path to becoming one of the best snipers in the Pacific theater proved to be a smooth one, despite his rocky entry into the Marine Corps. Arriving at Parris Island by bus, Ishkode had been shorn of his long black hair and issued uniforms. Physical training was easy for him, he'd been doing it all his life. But he really excelled when it came to rifle training. For the first time in his life he enjoyed the envy and praise of the white man. His instincts at hand-to-hand combat earned him even greater approval. Soon the men of his platoon not only looked up to him but sought him out for extra training and even advice. The camaraderie and near-adoration had changed Ishkode in ways that couldn't be measured.

Ready to do his duty to the best of his ability, Ishkode naturally wanted the best spotter available. "I want Two Bears." Two Bears was a member of the Cherokee tribe of Oklahoma and a flawless spotter, second only to Harold.

The captain had other ideas. "You got Ballard, Ishkode."

Ishkode was not pleased. "I thought you said I was the best."

"You are, Ishkode. And the best trainer, as well. If we get Karsten back, you'll be a team again. But right now, we need Ballard brought up to speed."

"Yes, sir," Ishkode grumbled.

Milbourn Ballard was the least respected man among the Marine sniper teams in Saipan. A mountain boy from North Carolina, Ballard received his first new pair of shoes on his arrival at boot camp. He was a crack shot at home, never missing a deer, turkey, possum, or revenuer for that matter.

But Ballard had a difficult time adapting to the rigid procedure required by the Marines. Recognizing his skill, the Marines designated him as a spotter in hopes he would someday turn out to be a highly-qualified shooter. That day had not yet come.

Ishkode found Ballard and gave him the news.

"I'm sure 'nough honored to partner up with you, Ishkode."

Ishkode narrowed his eyes and laid it out bluntly. "Don't be honored, be disciplined, for a change. From now on, you'll move when I say you can move, talk when I say you can talk, and do things the way you were taught at boot camp. This isn't Turkey Neck, North Carolina."

"I ain't from Turkey Neck, Chief." Though some thought Ballard dull, he was not. Recognizing Ishkode's sarcasm, he played along. "But I got kinfolk there. I get what you're saying, though. They can't shoot worth a damn."

"No need to worry about shooting, Ballard. The only thing you'll be shooting is the tin can from your C-rats. I'll be doing the shooting in this outfit."

"Oh, I know that. I just like to be ready...if 'n you was to get sick or drunk...or shot."

"I don't get sick, and I don't get drunk on duty. Or shot," Ishkode said firmly. "I recommend you do likewise. We're going out in about three days."

***

Ishkode and Milbourn Ballard had trudged twenty-five miles in the last thirty-six hours. Ishkode moved through the jungle silently, like a snake, whereas Ballard stumbled along like a drunken rhinoceros.

At chow and during rest periods, Ballard chattered away like a schoolgirl. Ishkode ignored him, but Ballard—who would happily talk to himself if no one else was around—kept up a steady barrage.

"You know, I ain't never had shoes before. Seems like these durn boots make an awful lot of noise...I'm used to sneaking up on stuff I want to shoot."

Ishkode was losing his patience. "Well, if you kept your trap shut, there would be less noise, I don't want the Japs all over us until after we do our damn job."

"I hear ya, Chief. But it just seems like I just always got a lot to say. Mama tells me I could talk the hind leg off a dog."

"Quit calling me Chief. It's Redmond, to you."

Once they neared their destination, they found a large tree, situated where they would have a view of a Japanese artillery emplacement. Their assignment was to take out the artillery spotters who had been targeting Allied forces with deadly accuracy. They scaled the tree and settled in. Ishkode counted five artillery pieces at the encampment, but it was up to him to determine who the two primary spotters were. Ishkode was given authority to take out more, if possible, but was told to "get those eagle-eyed Jap bastards at all costs."

Ishkode grabbed Ballard by the arm and whispered directly into his ear. "No jabbering in the hide."

"Right, Chief. I know when to shut up. Why, I once stood quiet for three hours, a-waitin' for a bear to come out of a cave. Course, the bear was noisy as hell, thrashing around and grunting. Lucky I had my old Springfield that day..."

Ballard's voice trailed off as Ishkode glared at him while giving a throat-slitting gesture.

Ishkode was more than irritated. This damn fool's gonna get us both greased. I'm gonna see that captain when I get back and tell him to stuff this clown back into his bibs and send him home to the hills where he can shoot possum and talk to himself as much as his damn fool ass likes. He looked around for a bit. Sure miss Harold. Guess I'll never hook up with a great spotter like him again.

Ishkode's thoughts were broken up by Ballard waving his hand in short circles. When he caught Ishkode's attention, he pointed to the artillery encampment. Japanese soldiers were moving the artillery pieces around and marshalling artillery shells next to their respective pieces. Efficient as always, the Japanese had all five weapons arranged and ready to go within minutes. They then stood at attention while two officers inspected each layout.

"We can nail 'em now!" Ballard whispered.

"I'll do the thinking around here, Ballard."

Ishkode wasn't about to concede anything to this cracked egg. The movement at the artillery base was likely a drill the Japs performed every day. Now that he'd seen the enemy's entire drill, he knew it would be a good opportunity to take out their spotters. Tomorrow when they trotted out their officers and cannon cockers, Ishkode would be ready. For now, they would wait.

CHAPTER 3

JUNE 1944

CHENGTU, CHINA

U.S. ARMY AIR FORCES 58TH BOMBARDMENT WING

"Well, Ray, your first wing command!" Major Henry Bohn of the United States Army Air Forces, 58th Bombardment Wing clapped Lt. Col. Montrell on the back.

Montrell was excited, but ready. "I never imagined I would be in charge of seventy-five birds."

"Why is that? You're one of the best!"

"I guess I just figured they'd keep me back in the States forever, training other pilots to take the fight to the Japs."

"What changed their minds?"

"I finally told them I was done. If I couldn't get my own plane into the skies, I was out. I knew they couldn't afford to let me go. And here I am. Still feels like a dream... or a nightmare, depending on how this mission goes."

"Yeah, speaking of...we better get these birds into the air."

It was mid-afternoon by the time seventy-five United States B-29 Superfortress bombers of the 58th Bombardment Wing lifted off from multiple bases in China. Newly pressed into service, B-29s had been arriving at bases in China for several months. After staging in India, they were flown over the Himalayan mountain range, affectionately referred to as "the hump." Their target was the Yawata area of Southern Japan where steel mills, oil refineries, and various other industrial facilities were located—in addition to a number of Japanese airfields. The United States was anxious to bring the war to the Japanese homeland. And the B-29 was the weapon they were counting on to bring Japan to its knees. Superseding the B-17 Flying Fortress, the B-29 Superfortress was a high-altitude, long-range bomber, capable of reaching targets 2,700 miles away. It could fly at altitudes in excess of 30,000 feet, requiring pressurized cabins, and carried a twenty-thousand-pound payload.

Flight Commander Montrell directed his aircraft's takeoff. "Increase throttle to one third."

"Throttle to one third," his copilot, Major Bohn, repeated.

"Flaps set to rise," Montrell commanded.

"Flaps set to rise."

The two men completed the takeoff procedure on the giant four-engine plane. As lead aircraft of the twelve-plane combat box formation, they assumed their position at 31,000 feet. The other pilots in the group aligned themselves on either side of the lead aircraft. For defensive purposes, the alignment provided visual access to every possible angle of attack as well as a shooting lane to those angles. Offensively, the combat box provided a concentration of bombs over the target area. Once in formation, the B-29s cruised at 220 miles per hour.

Superfortresses had three pressurized cabins. The bombardier sat in the forward compartment, all the way up front at the tip of the nose. Just behind him and slightly above sat the pilot and co-pilot. The flight engineer, radioman, and navigator stations were behind the pilot and copilot. A pressurized tunnel accessed the aft pressurized compartment, home of the central fire control gunner, the left and right gunners, and the radar man. The third pressurized compartment was small and not connected by a pressurized tunnel. It contained the tail gunner's position. During pressurized flight, the tail gunner was isolated and non-accessible. Although the crew members trained separately for their individual assignments, a complete crew normally stayed together throughout the campaign. Replacements would only come on board in cases of injury, illness, or death.

It was several hours before the group would arrive at the bomb target, so Montrell had plenty of time to deliberate. Always focused on the mission, he reviewed the three bombing runs they had previously executed in Thailand, destroying several Japanese outposts. Those missions were good shake-down cruises, as several mechanical problems had surfaced and been addressed. Montrell felt the B-29s were well vetted now, and he had no concerns—other than the amount of anti-aircraft fire and the number of Japanese fighters they might encounter at Yawata. He knew the B-29 was the best outfitted aircraft to deal with those obstacles. The eight Browning remote controlled machine guns and two 20mm M2 cannons in each airplane provided the means for defense.

Once they were in formation, Montrell and his crew executed the prescribed maneuvers that would ensure all systems were in operation prior to their bombing run.

"Open bomb bay doors," Montrell ordered.

"Bomb bay doors open," Bohn echoed.

"Close bomb bay doors."

"Doors closed."

"Tail guns execute run-out procedure."

The tail gunner and central gunner executed their run-out, and the M2 cannons went through a series of motions up and down, ending with the cannons firing two rounds straight down. The left and right gunners went through the same procedure. Every aircraft in the combat box and every aircraft in the entire group performed this same run-out within the next thirty minutes.

"Go to C-1," Montrell communicated to his group. Carrying out that command, all aircraft in the formation would fly on autopilot for the next several hours.

With no immediate tasks to perform, Montrell mentally reviewed the flight plan, step by step. His copilot assumed control of the cockpit while Montrell left to visit with the other crew members. He needed to check on the rear cannon system, as the central gunner and tail gunner reported a sensor light flashing on and off throughout the flight after the initial shake out. Montrell crawled through the pressurized connecting tunnel and maneuvered into the central compartment.

"What's up, Gunny?"

First Lieutenant Marvin Dobbs was the central gunner on Montrell's B-29 and was responsible for all defensive weapons systems on the aircraft. "We can't tell, sir. It's either a short in the sensor or a sticky valve. We're hoping a short in the sensor."

Dobbs had been in the Army Air Forces two years, but this was his first supervisory assignment. An African American whose crop-dusting father taught him how to fly at the age of twelve, Dobbs always dreamed of flying for the military.

Racial segregation placed him as a member of the Tuskegee Airmen, but he washed out of the program when it was discovered he had a minor heart condition.

Not to be put off, Dobbs applied for every other in-flight job. His determination landed him a position as a weapons control officer, where he certified on two heavy bombers. This was his second campaign, having already distinguished himself in B-24 Liberators in the skies over Tarawa.

"What about that damn computer?" Montrell asked.

"I don't believe the computer is the problem, Colonel. I hate to say it, but I'm leaning toward a valve problem, which would be the hardest to fix."

The B-29 bomber was a pioneer in the use of computers. Rudimentary though they were, five computers controlled the aircraft's weapon sighting system. They performed moderately well but were not popular with the old guard, ever suspicious of anything they couldn't control and didn't completely understand. Montrell was ready to give the on-board computers the benefit of the doubt but would have no trouble raising an objection should they cause any problems.

"Keep me appraised, Lieutenant. We don't want to go toe to toe with those Jap Zeros if any of our guns are disabled."

"Yes, sir. Will do, sir."

Montrell returned to the cockpit, checked the gauges, and gave his copilot, Major Bohn, an update. He then contacted the other pilots in his flight to get an update on their status. With no other issues in the foreground, he and Bohn discussed the weapons problem.

"Have you ever seen anything like that?" Bohn asked.

Montrell shook his head. "I've seen the gauges freeze, but this intermittent on-and-off shit is new to me. We aren't authorized to clear the cannons in this sector, so we'll probably have to wait until Yawata to check 'em out again. That isn't optimal, but we have no choice. Gunny is working on it. Let's see if he comes up with anything. You can take your break now and make the rounds. The men will be glad to see you."

"Yes, sir." Bohn stepped out of the cockpit.

Montrell checked the gauges once again and sat back. The B-29 added a new dimension to flying. Pressurized cockpits, sealed compartments, oxygen, computers, and a host of other new elements were now an everyday part of the United States Army Air Forces.

Montrell had come a long way from his early flying days. Raised on the family farm back in Ohio, Montrell earned his wings dusting his father's crops, along with many of his neighbors' fields as well. He laughed to himself, thinking how different those little bug smashers were, compared to the gigantic high-technology marvel he now commanded.

Between Montrell's desire to fly and his fervor against the Axis powers, he'd become a member of the Royal Canadian Air Force in 1939, instructing Canadian pilots who later found themselves in the Battle of Britain. Montrell desperately wanted to fly in combat, but the Canadians kept him tethered to the training role.

He was elated when he was finally able to join the U.S. Army Air Forces in 1942. He was certain he would soon find himself in the European or Pacific combat theater, flying in defense of his nation.

Unfortunately, he was unable to free himself from yet another training position, as he was too valuable as an instructor. He wrote letter after letter to his congressman, beseeching him for help in getting into a combat role in the war.

Later that same year, Montrell was assigned to the new Superfortresses, with orders to proceed to Boeing Field in Seattle, Washington, where he would train still others to fly the new aircraft and fight in the war. On arriving, Montrell insisted on an audience with his commander.

For the previous few years, pilot instructors were in short supply. The Civilian Pilot Training Program, though employed by both the Army Air Forces and the Navy for pilot training, was still less popular than having military flight instructors handling the job. Skilled flight instructors like Ray Montrell were valuable commodities and could demand certain perks in exchange for their services.

Ray insisted that he be given a combat slot after six months of training B-29 pilots. The Air Corps could not force Montrell to continue teaching if he chose not to, so his commander agreed to Montrell's "request." In six months he'd be given orders to a combat theater. In 1943

Montrell proceeded to Burma where he flew sorties and bombed Japanese targets in China and Indochina. He had finally gotten into the war.

Montrell's skill quickly earned him several promotions and the responsibility of wing command for his squadron. When the mission to start bombing Japan itself was formulated, Montrell was one of the first pilots selected. And now he found himself at the point of the sword, taking the fight to the Japs.

Montrell leaned forward and looked out the cockpit windows. He wasn't overly concerned with the defensive weapons issue on his aircraft as yet. He trusted the military technique of working the problem through logic and persistence until it was resolved. He approached issues the same way.

Bohn made it back to the copilot's seat. After hashing out the weapons problems and going over the mission with the rest of his squadron, Montrell settled into his thoughts. The B-29 aircraft he was flying was an awesome piece of technology—a weapons system envisioned, designed, and built by the best minds in the free world.

The mission: destroy Japan's ability to wage war. The method: drop 20,000 pounds of explosives from each of the seventy-five B-29s in the group.

Montrell had studied the target area well. He knew the location of each foundry and machine shop, along with the Japanese air fields and fuel depots.

Although hardened over several missions, Montrell also remembered something in the Intel photos that unsettled him. Homes, schools, and markets were adjacent to and in between the targets they would hit. Montrell wasn't a pacifist, he knew the best thing for everyone—Japanese included—would be a quick end to this vicious war. He also knew that the Japanese military had been merciless in their bombing and shelling, killing thousands of civilians in the process.

Still, he couldn't help thinking about his own wife and family back in Ohio. What if they were targeted by enemy bombers? How would he feel? A chill went through him like a knife. He couldn't get the sight out of his head... his wife and child running in terror as bombs exploded all around them.

Only when Henry Bohn brought his attention to a mission bench mark did those horrible sights leave him.

CHAPTER 4

"These are the new men, Dante?"

"They are, Captain Drummond. Privates Wilke, Johnson, and Ryzbicki."

"Welcome to Alpha Company, men." The captain liked to meet the replacement soldiers and make sure everyone was in tune with the strategy laid out for the reconnaissance teams of the 82nd Airborne. "Whatever you learned before your arrival, you'll find that we follow the book here...except when we don't."

Drummond paused and looked around, making eye contact with each of the new men. "When we first embarked on this mission several weeks ago, our rifle squads were looking for hardened German bunkers. After a number of ambushes, botched patrols, and dead soldiers, we've learned that the Jerries are not all in permanent, hardened bunkers. Most of our enemy contact thus far has been against small mobile units using hit-and-run tactics. Our mission to clear defensive bunkers ahead of the big assault force has been stifled significantly by their tactics. In response, we've set up hunter-killer squads to find these small units, engage, and eliminate them—as many of them as possible. Your squad is such a unit. This mission is critical to the success of the Allied effort to chase these damn Krauts back to Germany."

32

That elicited shouts and cheers.

"Listen to your squad leaders and support them. Sergeant Crucianelli and Corporal Hester have all my confidence and support." Captain Drummond glared directly at Virgil Shields, causing Shields to squirm uncomfortably.

When the captain left, Dante went over the procedures again. The new men were quiet, no doubt scared to death before their first patrol.

"All right, let's move out!" Dante ordered.

The squad moved rapidly for five miles before stopping for a short break.

Hester spoke with the men in subdued tones. "In a couple of miles, we'll be near the last ambush site. We won't expect any Jerries to be hanging around, but we are moving into the area where they've been very active. Remember our procedure, once we find a ripe area, we establish a skirmishing line. We then move out at a slow pace for one hour. If we don't establish contact, we form up in patrol file and move on to another area of known or suspected activity. Any questions?"

Shields spoke up. "I want point."

Dante and Hester looked at each other and then Dante addressed the men. "Shields will hold point until we hit the hot area and form our skirmishing line. The Jerries could be anywhere around from this point on, so we'll slow our pace and be observant. If we see signs of the enemy, we'll move into the skirmishing line formation sooner. Any questions or issues?"

Wilke, one of the new men, was having problems. "I got the goddamn shits, Sarge," He had ducked out of the patrol several times to relieve himself, running to catch up to the squad each time.

"When did it start?" Dante asked.

"Before we left this morning...I know, I should have spoken up."

"Damn right you should've spoken up. Now you've

jeopardized the mission and put every man in your squad at risk. You think you're George Fucking Patton that we can't get along without you?"

"I'm sorry, Sarge. I'm sorry." Wilke shook like a scared puppy.

Dante and Hester huddled to discuss the situation. "We're gonna have to leave you here, Wilke," Hester said. "You won't be worth a damn in a fight, and you'll slow us up as well. It's too risky to send you back on your own, so we'll leave you with a canteen and some chuck. You sit tight and we'll pick you up on the way back. You'll have to find your own shit paper."

Wilke nodded and stepped out. The squad formed up and went on in pursuit of the Germans. Dante didn't like leaving a man behind, but it was more important to accomplish their mission.

As they trudged along he mused about Shields. That bastard had guts. He had proved that in earlier missions. I guess the only thing Shields hates more than dagos are Krauts. Well, I'll give him every chance he wants to take them out...as long as it benefits the mission.

***

Virgil Shields fell back from his position on point. "There's sign everywhere, Crucianelli, it's time to form those skirmishing lines."

"Are we dealing with more machine-gun nests or have they moved other units in?" Dante asked.

"I've seen no sign of heavy weapons, but I'm starting to see what appears to be a double column of infantry crisscrossing the area. I think they're looking for us."

"Let's see if we can't help 'em find us." Dante formed the men into a double skirmishing line, with the second line staggered behind the first.

"Ready hand grenades!" he instructed the second line. "All out and move at half-pace." The squad moved forward.

"Watch for tripwires and booby traps," Hester muttered.

Within fifteen minutes, one of the new men stopped and held up his arm.

Hester acknowledged the solider. "What do you see, Ryzbicki?"

Ryzbicki stood as still as a statue, pointing down with his other arm. Partially hidden under the brush, a heavy wire stretched out, visible for thirty or forty feet.

Hester and Shields followed the wire in one direction, Crucianelli the other. Every ten feet or so they found a Stielhandgranate, the common German hand grenade with a long wooden throwing handle, buried just below the surface of the ground.

"You men all come up and look at this," Cru ordered. "We're probably gonna see a lot more of this shit, and it's best you know what to look for."

After the men filed past, Cru issued orders, "Form up in a double column again. Hester, you take point with Shields. We'll need an extra set of eyes from here on out."

"Where do you think these birds went?" Hester asked.

"They're probably looking for a unit larger than our squad. I'm thinking they're traveling perpendicular to our position now. We're gonna give 'em a surprise."

Thirty minutes later Hester hustled back. "We found 'em, Danny. There's at least thirty men planting more of those damn tripwire booby traps just ahead."

Dante nodded. "We're gonna let 'em lay one of those lines, Hester, but in the middle of their work we'll give them a little surprise. They won't be able to run without setting their own traps off. Get Shields back here."

After Shields and Hester returned, the squad worked its way forward until they spotted the Germans laying two booby trap lines. While the enemy worked, Dante positioned two men on each side, surrounding the Germans.

"Now!" Dante yelled. Each squad member threw a grenade at the Germans, killing a few immediately and wounding several others. The remaining Germans panicked and ran every which way, setting off their own grenades. Within minutes every enemy soldier was down.

Dante's squad worked its way across the area, disarming the remaining traps and taking anything of value.

***

Captain Drummond had summoned Crucianelli again.

"Good job once again, Dante. You better watch it or General Eisenhower's going to put you in charge of the whole damn works."

"Thank you, sir, but the credit belongs to Private Shields and Corporal Hester. They made this operation click."

Drummond looked surprised. "So you and Shields have smoked the peace pipe?"

"I wouldn't say that, sir. But I will give him credit for a job well done. In spite of our personal disagreements, Shields is a damn good soldier."

"That's one of the strengths of a good NCO, Dante. Being able to get the best out of your men, despite personality conflicts that may be in play."

"Thank you, sir."

"Any other issues I should know about?" Drummond asked.

"A slight shit problem, but we handled it."

Drummond raised an eyebrow. "Now you have my interest."

Dante suppressed a smile. "One of the new guys got the shits but waited to tell us until after we covered some ground. We told him to stay put while we finished the mission and picked him up on our way back."

"I presume he was okay?"

"Other than bleeding from wiping his ass on leaves and reeds. He'll survive, sir."

Drummond shook his head and pointed to a map pinned to the wall of his tent. "The troops have moved off Omaha and the other beaches and will soon be at our position in strength. The Jerries will either be slaughtered or forced to move back. We're going to be chasing the ones that move back. Their reinforcements won't get here for several weeks. When they do arrive, the main forces behind us will take them on, and I expect we'll be dropped somewhere else behind the lines. For now, we continue to seek out and identify German defensive—and offensive—units. Tomorrow at nine-hundred hours, a convoy will pick us up and carry us fifty miles further in. I'm going to put you in charge of the whole platoon. Can you handle that, Crucianelli?"

Dante thought about it a moment and nodded. "I believe I can, sir. Do you want the platoon to continue operating in squads or go to platoon level?"

"I think that will best be determined after we get our feet wet. We'll go out in squads at first and sniff the air. Then we'll have a better idea." Drummond cocked his head and looked at Dante. "Normally a platoon is handled by a first or second looey. Unfortunately, they're all getting killed. You're going to be a noncom in that position, so watch yourself. Some of the men will try to butt heads with you." Drummond smiled. "I don't want to promote you to second lieutenant until they start living longer."

"Thank you, sir. I'll do my best to comply with that."

Chapter 5

Ishkode spent an hour watching the Japanese artillery encampment through Ballard's scope. The cool mist of early morning fogged the lens. Every few minutes, he wiped the moisture off. Ballard was still asleep. When his snores started sounding like a chainsaw, Ishkode reached over and shook him awake.

"Damn, Chief! You almost knocked me outta the tree!"

"You were snoring loud enough to expose our position to the whole damn Jap army."

"Sorry, Chief. You know, once I fell asleep in deer camp and sawed so damn loud that the boys tossed me out into the snow. I had to make breakfast every day as punishment and..." Ballard stopped.

Glaring, Ishkode once again drew his index finger across his neck.

"Sorry," Ballard whispered sheepishly.

The rest of the morning went by without incident. The two took turns watching through Ballard's scope, hoping the Japs would put on another parade-ground drill like they had the day before. Around 1400 hours, activity in the Japanese encampment accelerated. Sure enough, the two officers trotted out as their men moved the artillery pieces and shells around in snapping fashion.

"Which officer you gonna nail first?" Ballard whispered, trying Ishkode's patience once again.

"Do you remember our orders and our discussion?" Ishkode whispered.

Ballard looked puzzled. "We're supposed to take out the two best artillerymen. But how can we tell which officers are best?"

"Ballard, how many officers have you seen firing artillery pieces?"

"Sorry, Chief, I remember now. We have to take out the shooters themselves. How we gonna know which Japs are which? We haven't seen them shoot."

"Look through that scope of yours. The Japs are prideful and vain. They usually wear some type of colored rope or patch if they've earned bragging rights. Should only be a couple that are shooting as accurately as we've been led to believe."

Ballard peered through his scope from group to group. "Think I found 'em. The one with the pointy hat has two yellow stars on his sleeve. The one with the scar on his face has three."

"Let me have that scope." From his pre-mission briefings, Ishkode confirmed what Ballard had seen. "Those are the ones." Once he had the locations, he handed the scope back to Ballard. "I'm going to shoot the one with the three stars first, then the other. Remember our egress drill and don't fuck it up!"

"Yes, sir."

Ishkode set up his rifle scope based on the distance and wind. Ballard observed through his own scope. The first shot cracked off and the artilleryman with three yellow stars on his sleeve collapsed like a steer hit with a sledge hammer. A split second later, Ishkode's second shot hit the two-star artilleryman, who crumpled in a heap next to his comrade.

"You got 'em both. Great shots, Chief!"

The remaining Japanese soldiers froze. Then the camp erupted like a swarm of angry bees. Officers screamed and waved their arms. Soldiers started shooting in the direction of Ishkode's tree, and others prepped the heavy machine guns.

Before the first shots hit the vegetation around them, Ishkode and Ballard were packed up, down the tree, and running on their predetermined exit route. The heavy machine gun commenced, splintering small trees all around them. Ballard let out a howl and skidded to the ground like a runner stealing third base face down.

"Where're you hit?" Red yelled, snatching Ballard up off the ground while still on the run.

"My left shoulder. Feels like a damn wheelbarrow went through it."

"We've got to run at least fifteen minutes before we're far enough away from these fuckers, Ballard. Make yourself run."

"Wait! I dropped my scope. I gotta go back."

"Fuck the scope! We can get another one. Move your feet, you damn ridge runner, or I'll shoot you myself."

***

"Another job well done, Ishkode." Out of respect, Captain Andersen made it a point to address Ishkode Redmond by his given name—not Chief or Cody or even Red, for that matter. He felt Ishkode deserved that respect as a human being, not just for the excellent job he always did. "That Japanese artillery unit fired for two hours yesterday and all they managed to kill was a bunch of damn monkeys and lizards. Headquarters wanted to let you know they appreciate your work. How's Ballard doing?"

Ishkode hadn't always gotten respect as a result of his ethnic background, and although he didn't pitch a bitch over it, he appreciated it whenever someone held him in high regard for how he carried himself and for what he achieved. Ishkode especially liked the captain.

"Thanks, Captain. Ballard's doing okay. That ridge-runner is one tough son of a bitch. Don't think he'll be climbing any trees for a while, though. When can you find me another spotter?"

"We've got a different assignment for you, Ishkode. On this one you won't be able to use a spotter. The Japanese brain trust on Saipan is headquartered in a small mountain about halfway across the island. They're at an elevation of around twelve-hundred feet, and the approach to their position is a sheer vertical cliff."

"How do they get in and out, sir?"

"Have you ever seen a helicopter, Ishkode?"

"No, I haven't, sir. Is that what the Japs are using?"

"Sort of. They have these tiny aircraft called autogyros that can get them in and out of their little rat's nest up there. The damn things look like they were designed just for that purpose. They only need ninety feet to take off. It just so happens that the Air Corps shot one down a couple weeks ago. It wasn't much more than a rough landing, so they have it up and running again."

Ishkode thought he knew where the captain was going with this. "And I bet we're planning to sneak into their little lair with that thing."

"Yes, we are. I'm sending you over to the Air Corps unit that has the autogyro. We'll need you to learn as much about the little bugger as you can—and you'll also have to learn how to fly it."

This caught Ishkode off guard. "I'll do whatever is necessary, sir. But may I ask why it will be necessary for me to fly it?"

Repositioning himself, the captain stared at the ground, failing to meet Ishkode's eyes. "The Japs have killed many of the Chamorro natives on this island, so naturally the natives hate them. We've recruited many of them ourselves, and they've helped us a great deal with mapping and things like that. They've also been used in the same capacity as you...as snipers. Their knowledge of the land and their hatred for the Japs makes them good candidate for the task. They're not particularly skilled shooters, but when they get close enough, they're effective. One job we've given them is sitting at the floor of the mountain and shooting these little autogyros down. They shoot the pilot, leaving the passenger sitting there with his dick in his hand. We'll do our best to alert them of your mission, but communication with them is never a given. If something happens to your pilot, you'll have a better chance of survival if you can gain control of the aircraft."

Ishkode took it all in stride. "Right...and who's the target, sir?"

"Everyone's heard of General Yoshitsugu Saito, the man in charge of the Japanese Saipan contingent." Andersen looked at Ishkode for confirmation.

"Yes, sir."

"Well, Saito may be the head Jap, but he's not the operational guy. That's the guy we want. And as much as I hate to say it, the son of a bitch is doing a damn good job. His name is Colonel Hisao Niwa."

"And I take it he's he up in the cave, sir?"

"I think he and Saito are both there at times, but we know Niwa's there. And he provides us with a great opportunity. Niwa, it seems, likes to walk. When he's not working, he hikes back and forth from one end of the cave to the other. He walks for a couple hours at a time and arrives at the front of the cave every thirty-three minutes. He takes a couple of deep breaths of the fresh mountain air and back into the cave he goes."

"How long is he out there?"

Andersen knew that presented a problem. "Only about six or seven minutes, but that's not the real problem. He mixes it up. Sometimes he walks in the morning, other times in the afternoon or evening."

"How do we know about all these walks and the timing? Who came up with that information, sir?"

"That's interesting as well. The Japanese aren't totally self-sufficient up in that cave. Some of the native people they've been preying on have been abducted and forced to work for them as domestic servants. Many have tried to escape and have been shot for their efforts. But several have made it out, sneaking down the mountain at night. We've interviewed them extensively. And we've even gotten a few to go back up and spy for us. It's dangerous for them, but they've seen their families and friends murdered by the Japs and feel they have nothing to lose. They want revenge."

"When do I hook up with these autogyro people, Captain?"

"Be ready to leave tomorrow. A C-47 is coming in at eleven hundred hours to pick you up."

**

Ishkode spent a week at the Saipan U.S. Air Corps field learning how to fly the small autogyro that would be used in an attempt to assassinate Colonel Niwa. He reviewed photos of Niwa and other top commanders who occupied the mountain stronghold. Redmond had been advised to seek out additional targets of opportunity during the mission, should conditions allow. He was paired up with one of the Saipan snipers who had been shooting at the autogyros ever since the Japanese had taken up residency in the mountain.

"Are you sure your name isn't Ballard?" Ishkode asked.

"No, no Master Ishkode. My name Mata," the diminutive Chamorro man replied.

"And I told you to stop calling me master," Ishkode scolded.

The two had been working together for most of the week, pulling reconnaissance on the mountain hideout whenever Ishkode wasn't training on the autogyro. Mata proved to be an excellent tracker and observer, and not a bad shot either. His propensity to jabber nonstop, however, irritated the quiet Ojibwa. All day long, Mata muttered away in Chamorro, injecting a few words of English here and there.

"It chow time yet, master?" Mata asked.

Starving since the Japanese invasion, the local natives relished the C-rations the U.S. military routinely doled out to them.

Redmond scowled. "If you keep pissing me off, I'm going to feed you to the sharks."

Mata smiled from ear to ear. "Shark no eat Mata. Mata too skinny, maybe like American Indian better!"

"Indian would smoke a shark over a slow fire."

The two men bantered while they ate lunch. Then the conversation turned serious as they planned their upcoming mission. They both anticipated difficulties as a result of the limited time frame in the air waiting for Niwa to show himself. Ishkode had an idea which he felt might have a pretty good chance of success. He hoped to address it with Captain Andersen as soon as possible.

CHAPTER 6

YAWATA, JAPAN

U.S. ARMY AIR FORCES 58TH BOMBARDMENT WING

Lieutenant Colonel Montrell prepped his flight as they neared Yawata under cover of darkness.

The B-29s' primary targets were the iron and steel works, along with the nearby coke plants that provided their fuel. It was now night and each B-29 would bomb individually rather than in flight formation.

Yawata boasted thirty-five Kawasaki twin-engine fighters and twenty Kawasaki single-engine fighters to protect it. The area was also defended by anti-aircraft and barrage balloons. The intent was that the barrage balloons, launched with heavy cables hanging from them, would either collide with the incoming bombers or damage them.

As Montrell's flight entered the air space over the city, darkened by the blackout order, anti-aircraft-fire burst below them. The B-29s were too high for it to be effective. The flight, now lined up like taxis at an airport, went in one by one over the targeted areas and released their bombs. The majority of the Japanese fighter aircraft protecting Yawata remained on the ground. Later Montrell learned that previous battle damage and lack of maintenance components had grounded them. The few that were able to take to the air buzzed around ineffectually, unable to get past the defensive guns of the B-29s.

One enemy fighter targeted Montrell's B-29, approaching from behind. Montrell and his copilot held their breath as Lieutenant Dobbs and his crew mate attempted to fire the rear cannons.

Despite their efforts, only one of the rear cannons was operational, and even it was not firing up to speed, allowing the Japanese fighter to press his attack.

Montrell executed a steep dive and hard turn. The Japanese pilot reacted to the maneuver quickly, which placed his aircraft within the sights of the B-29's top and side gunners who shot up the Japanese fighter plane as if it were a tin coffee can.

"Got 'em!" Bohn shouted. "Great shooting, men!"

All the men on board cheered as flaming fragments of the Japanese fighter swirled down toward the ground. Their glee ended abruptly as intense anti-aircraft fire burst furiously all around them. Montrell's successful evasive maneuver had brought the B-29 within range of the ack-ack guns on the ground.

"Let's get her up, Henry!" Montrell shouted.

Before Montrell and Bohn were able to get the aircraft out of range, an anti-aircraft shell burst near the rear of the aircraft, sending shrapnel through the tail section and rear gun module. The B-29 started shaking like a dog in the rain as the two men struggled to control the plane.

"Hang on!" Montrell shouted, fighting to regain control. After losing more altitude for a short time, he and Bohn managed to pull the aircraft out of the dive and stabilize it.

"All systems: check!" Montrell ordered. "Checking, sir," Bohn responded.

"Checking, sir," Dobbs echoed.

The side gunners and top gunners responded as well, but the rear gunner in the damaged module remained silent.

After a short pause, Montrell personally called out the rear gunner. "Sergeant Williams? Sergeant Williams!"

There was no response.

Montrell radioed the second pilot in command and reported the damage. "You have the squadron now, Bob. Take her home."

"Will do, sir," Major Robert Whittaker acknowledged. "Can we provide you with an escort?"

"No, Bob, we'll be okay. As soon as we are good and clear of the fighters and ack-ack, we'll take her under twelve thousand and keep her under a hundred and seventy knots. We'll be bringing up the rear. Keep our breakfast warm for us."

"Will do, sir...and Godspeed."

***

After thirty minutes, Montrell took the aircraft down in altitude. Only then would they be able to access the rear gunner station to check on Sergeant Williams without requiring pressurization. The entire crew performed their duties in silence, concerned about their comrade.

"Eight thousand feet, Colonel," the copilot reported. "Pressure off," Montrell ordered. "I'm going through the tunnel."

He left his seat and crawled to the aft compartment. There he was joined by Lieutenant Dobbs, carrying the first aid kit. They moved toward the tail and opened the access door leading to the tail gunner's station. Although a veteran of many air campaigns, Dobbs gasped.

A large piece of shrapnel had pierced the rear gun compartment just below the gunner's viewing window, passing completely through the compartment and Sergeant Williams. His body was nearly cut in half.

Montrell placed his hand on Dobbs' shoulder, and both men remained silent for a moment. Cold air passed through the entrance and exit holes made by the shrapnel, whistling loudly.

"Let's get him out of there."

The two men attempted to open the gun compartment door, but the shrapnel had jammed the latch mechanism. After several attempts, Dobbs gave up.

"Colonel, we're going to need a torch to cut it open." "I hate to leave him here like this Gunny."

Dobbs nodded. "I'll stay here with him until he's removed and his remains can be cared for in a proper manner." "Thanks, Gunny. I'll let the others know what happened." Montrell crawled back through the tube and returned to his pilot's seat. He nodded to Bohn and picked up the intercom.

"This is Colonel Montrell. Our comrade and brother-in-arms, Sergeant Richard Williams, was killed by the ack-ack shrapnel. Lieutenant Dobbs will stay with him until we land. Anyone who wishes may go back and pay their respects as duty allows."

The com went silent for a moment. "We will miss Sergeant Williams. His family and friends can take pride in knowing that his passing was not in vain. His efforts greatly assisted our mission in taking the fight to the Japanese homeland. God bless Sergeant Williams, and God bless America."

CHAPTER 7

S ergeant Dante Crucianelli had spent two days preparing for the mission assigned to his newly acquired platoon. His initial briefing with the men had gone well, with the exception of the always cantankerous Virgil Shields. Unlike previous disagreements, however, Shields did not object to Dante's abilities, but rather the mission as assigned.

The plan called for the forty-man platoon to move out in eight squads of five. They were to move rapidly until they reached the front where they had operated in the campaign to this point. They would then proceed at half speed until contact was made with Germans or German booby traps.

"How the hell will one squad know where any other squad is?" Shields wanted to know.

"Do you have a suggestion, Corporal?" Dante asked Shields, who had been promoted based on Crucianelli's recommendation after their last mission.

Shields gave his assessment freely and bluntly, as always. "Move out in platoon formation till we hit the frontier. Why waste time dawdling through shit we already cleared out?

Dante didn't disagree with Shield's position, as he'd thought the same thing when he first saw the plan. Captain

Drummond had indicated he didn't care if Dante changed it, so long as the mission succeeded. If it failed as a result of Dante's tinkering, however, Dante would own it.

Dante nodded and looked at Hester. "What's your opinion?"

"I agree with Shields on this. Why crack eggs when we've already made the omelet?"

Dante and Shields both gave Hester a curious look. Hester tried to explain. "I'm just sayin'—"

Holding up his hand, Dante laughed. "I get it Hester, and I agree with you both. We'll insert a little creative thinking here." He looked around. "Second platoon, on your feet. Form up in platoon columns. We should reach our area of expected engagement tomorrow around mid-morning. Shields, will you take point?"

"Who else? I sure as hell don't want anyone else up there."

The men formed up in a double column and proceeded at quick step. They encountered no German activity throughout the day and stopped at 1900 hours to set up their bivouac in the middle of a draw, just below the crest of a small hill.

Crucianelli directed the activities. "Pitch the tents well away from those trees, we don't want any Krauts sneaking up on us through the damn woods. Set up the Browning on the north perimeter."

After the men staked out a rough perimeter, Hester assigned the night watch. "Two men on watch at all times, all night, two hours shifts. One mans the Browning, the other walks the perimeter."

Shields was always ready for action. "I'll take first shift."

"Fine. Pick your partner. The rest of you men partner up and choose a shift. Coordinate with Shields. Whoever doesn't get a night watch digs the latrine pit or cleans the Browning and sets it up."

The Browning .30 caliber machine gun, used by most infantry units in World War II, was a valuable field weapon. However, if not cleaned every day, it had a tendency to jam up. Hester repeated the often-heard training mantra. "A jammed-up weapon is your worst enemy."

After the platoon readied for night duties, Crucianelli was satisfied. "Okay, let's break out the chow and fill our bellies."

***

Three days later, while operating in Orleans Province, Dante's platoon was hit. The explosion took out half of an eight-man squad. Two were killed immediately. Two more were badly wounded. A German heavy machine gun opened up on the adjacent squad as soon as the booby trap went off. Men screamed, yelled, and ran.

"Fall back and return fire! Fall back and return fire!" Dante yelled.

The more seasoned veterans of the campaign dropped back, took cover, and fired on the German machine-gun nest. About a dozen men, mostly rookies, fled in panic. Crucianelli had no choice but to let them go until the gun was neutralized. Disaster struck again when Crucianelli sent a squad to flank the gun from the rear, as they had done before with success. Lying in wait, another enemy gun position decimated them and then opened up on the remaining squads in the platoon.

Shields scurried over to Dante's position. "We're getting slaughtered here. We can't pull back and we can't move up. Better come up with something, Crucianelli."

"Where's Dingman?" Crucianelli shrugged. "What the fuck does that matter?"

"Just get Dingman over here right away—if he's still alive, that is."

Ten minutes later Shields and Dingman jumped into Dante's shallow foxhole.

"Dingman, you see where that German gun is?" Dante pointed.

Dingman was a bit nervous, but not shaken, "Yeah, I see it."

"You think you can put a grenade in the middle of that bunch?" Dante knew Dingman had played professional baseball in the States—a center fielder noted for throwing runners out at home all the way from midfield.

Dingman thought about it a second. "I reckon I can." "Okay, take this grenade, pull the pin, and wait till the count of four. Then fire it in there."

Dingman took the grenade and pulled the pin. Just as Dante reached the count of four, Dingman stood up and threw the grenade at the machine-gun nest, which was still spitting out fire. The grenade detonated—and the gun went silent.

"Damn, you got 'em!" Shields shook his fist in triumph.

"Can you see the other one?" Dante turned to Dingman.

"Yeah, it's about thirty yards farther back, I think I can hit it, though."

"Okay, same drill. But this time throw it on the count of three."

Dingman took another grenade, pulled the pin, and waited for the count of three. He jumped up, wound up, and threw the grenade at the nest. The grenade detonated, silencing that machine gun as well.

Shields pounded Dingman on his back. "You got that one, too, Dingman. Damn!"

"Best center fielder in the majors!" Dante gave him a thumbs up and turned to the other men. "Second platoon, form up! Shields, find Hester, check those nests, and make sure they're all dead. The rest of you find our wounded and render aid."

Dante used several seasoned veterans to form a squad to locate the men who panicked and ran off when the fighting started. "Those fuckers will get every shit detail from here on out."

In the following three days, Dante's team took out seven additional German machine gun crews and five German mortar teams.

***

"Damn! Dingman the center fielder," Captain Drummond repeated. "That was one hell of a mission, Dante."

"I'm just glad we found most of the men who ran off."

"I'm sure if we'd had time to properly train them they wouldn't have bugged out like that. And I'm truly sorry about Hester. He was a good man and I know you two were close."

"Thank you, Captain. The other two who were killed ran right into a German machine gun nest after they panicked. A damn shame. And yes, Hester was a good man. I'll miss him. He died trying to save those two. I think he deserves a Silver Star, sir."

"I'll send it up the chain, Dante. I understand Shields performed above and beyond again, as well."

"He did, sir. The third day of our patrol, Shields discovered a booby trap field. At great personal risk, he stopped two squads before they stumbled into the area."

"I'm putting him in for a bronze, Dante...and you as well. You've cleared out a large area, allowing our advancing columns to challenge the Hun counteroffensive unfettered. I'm very proud of this group of men."

"Thank you, Captain."

Drummond gestured to a folding chair next to a table which the staff had been using for operational charting. "Sit down, Dante. How about a hot cup of joe? It isn't very fresh but it's damn hot most of the time."

"Thank you, sir."

"How's the family Dante? Any more siblings back there or still holding at fourteen?"

Dante laughed. "Still fourteen, Captain, and chow hounds everyone. Good thing three of us are in the service—makes it go a little farther."

"I bet your mom can't wait for all of you to go home."

"Yes, sir. She's worried I guess."

"And your Uncle Silvio...bet he wishes you were back. From the driving I saw you doing earlier I bet all the fruit and vegetables you delivered got to the customer before it was even picked."

"Well, that's how we made our money, sir. The freshest produce hooked the biggest customers and kept 'em coming back."

"I want very much want for you to see that great family again, Dante."

Not knowing where this was going, Dante squirmed in his seat a bit. "Yes, sir."

"You've performed every mission brilliantly. Some of the things you've done defy explanation. And while I appreciate your success very much—as does upper command—I also have to caution you."

"Sir?"

"You have not risked the lives of your men unnecessarily, and that is very good considering the degree of your success. But even though I'm stuck back here in operations too damn much, I do have ears. I happen to know that on several occasions you have put yourself at great personal risk for the sake of the mission."

"Isn't that what we're here for, Captain?"

Drummond didn't disagree. "It is, but I also want to advise you of something. It's going to be a long war. We have many more missions to complete before this Nazi menace has been dealt with. You will provide a better service to your country if you stay healthy and fit for the duration of that campaign. If you get killed or wounded, you won't be of any more use to the great cause we have undertaken."

"I'll try to keep that in mind sir, I don't want to let my country down."

Drummond put his hand on Dante's shoulder. "Good, because I'd also miss you, you damn Italian tomato picker. Now get the hell out of here."

"Thank you, sir... I would miss you also."

Dante saluted, shook Drummond's hand, and departed to resume his duties.

CHAPTER 8

At his next briefing with Captain Andersen, Ishkode outlined a plan he felt had a better chance of succeeding in taking out Colonel Niwa. Instead of trying to shoot Niwa from the autogyro while the colonel was taking one of his walks, Ishkode and Mata would land the gyro and enter the cave themselves. With a little makeup and a uniform, Ishkode could pass himself off as a Japanese soldier. Mata would pose as a domestic servant.

Captain Andersen shook his head. "I don't know, Ishkode. This sounds risky."

"If things go to hell, we'll shoot our way out of the cave and get the hell out of there."

Andersen wasn't convinced. "You'll have no backup in the cave, and...well...if you fail and get killed, we won't be able to use the autogyro again."

"There's that chance." Ishkode agreed. "But as it stands right now, it may be weeks before we get a shot at Niwa. Plus, if my plan works, we might get a shot at Saito and other prime targets up there as well."

"Is this Mata a Steady Eddie?"

"He is, sir. I've worked with many men in the Marines and I have as much confidence in him as I do in some of the best men I know. And he's fighting for his homeland."

"What do you need from me?" Andersen asked, somewhat reluctantly.

"Besides authorization, we'll need a Japanese officer's uniform that fits me. We'll also need a Japanese officer's pistol. I believe they carry the Nambu T14. And I'll need five extra magazines. I'll work with Mata on the plan and let you know if there's anything else."

Captain Andersen was grateful he had a man like Ishkode, who was not only efficient at his job, but a creative thinker. "I like you, Ishkode...on a personal level as well as professional. I don't want to lose you as a military asset or a friend. Your plan calls for the natives who've been shooting at the Japanese autogyros to shoot at you and Mata..."

"But without that activity, the Japanese will be suspicious."

"You know from experience it's hard to control those shooters," the captain warned. "Trying to explain to them to shoot toward the autogyro, but not the occupants in it will be a gamble."

"Mata thinks he can take care of that end of it, sir. I believe him. And maybe we could have a few Marines at the base to ride herd or do the 'shooting.'"

"My other concern is the colonel. You know he's a 'by the book' man. He's not going to take to this plan readily. He'd just as soon have the Navy let loose with their big guns on that cave. I can just hear him. 'Seal the damn thing off, starve the bastards. Don't go fiddle fucking around in there.'"

"And when the Navy tried that before, they killed a lot of Saipan natives, didn't they, sir?"

Andersen nodded. "Yes, they did, but there's nothing the colonel—or the admiral either, for that matter—would like better than to level the whole damn mountain. There's a big plan for Saipan, Ishkode. I'm not at liberty to share it at this time, but the sooner every single Jap on this island is killed or captured, the sooner that big plan can be implemented. And I assure you, neither the colonel nor the admiral will risk their necks on a plan that may not succeed and could slow down that operation."

***

Two days later, Ishkode and Mata crept within fifty yards of the base of the mountain that contained the Japanese operational command of Saipan. Mata knew many of the routes used by the Saipan natives who escaped from their Japanese prison cave. Ishkode felt it would be good to have several avenues of escape after completing their mission. He also felt there was a good chance the autogyro would either be put out of commission by the Japanese or inaccessible to him and Mata.

The Japanese hadn't ignored the problem of escaping prisoners. They blocked the routes with large boulders. They also lit the area with several spotlights powered by gasoline generators. Sentries patrolled the mouth of the cave. Thanks to their German allies, the sentries were accompanied by German Shepherd dogs.

Ishkode made drawings of everything he could see and took notes as well. Mata, with his old British Enfield rifle, kept watch.

"I shoot Jap tonight, master?"

Ishkode gave him an angry look. "You shoot that damn gun and I'll torture you myself—if we live long enough, that is. You keep a lookout for the Japs. But if any of them need shooting, I'll be the one doing it."

Ishkode had left his sniper rifle in camp. In place of it, he carried an M3A1 grease gun. Back at camp Mata had watched Ishkode firing the weapon. The M3A1, manufactured by General Motors, was an effective close-quarters weapon. Though only twenty-nine inches long and weighing eight pounds, it fired .45 caliber bullets accurately for almost one hundred yards. It fired at the rate of 450 rounds per minute and had a standard 30-round magazine.

Ishkode had already qualified on every infantry weapon

in the U.S. Marine Corps arsenal and was skilled with each. As Mata stood in awe, Ishkode shredded tree stumps into match sticks as smoothly and efficiently as if he'd been born with the weapon in his hand.

"Please? I shoot gun, master?"

"You keep your hands off of my weapon, Mata. Stick to that chunk of iron you drag around with you, in case we need to shoot any elephants or rhinoceroses."

Mata was puzzled. "Is rhinoceroses a Japanese soldier man?"

Ishkode chuckled. "No, it's a giant animal with a big horn. It would feed your village for a week."

"I see rhinoceros, I shoot, master!"

"Good. Now just shut up and let me finish mapping this damn mountain."

"No need map. Mata know all ways up, all ways down. When we eat?"

"Damn, you ate all of our C-rats on the way here.

Where the hell do you put it?" "I put in stomach, master."

Before Ishkode could respond, a hand-held light from a Japanese patrol shined on their position. Ishkode and Mata hit the dirt. The Japanese patrol started yelling and shooting at them. Before the Japs could sharpen their aim, however, Ishkode trained his grease gun on them, taking out three soldiers in rapid order. Quick as a whip, Mata shot two more with his old Enfield. What was left of the patrol stayed hidden as Ishkode and Mata beat a hasty retreat. They ran about a mile through the heavy jungle without stopping. When they finally stopped, Ishkode noticed that Mata was bleeding from the calf of his left leg.

Mata didn't want to bother with his minor injury. "No hurt bad...we go quick."

Ishkode ignored him, quickly wrapping his leg. Like all U.S. Marines, Ishkode carried the standard M-2 Individual Jungle Medical Kit. It was small enough to hang from either a cartridge belt or a pistol, and in addition to rudimentary medical supplies it also carried a remedy for Athlete's Foot and water purification tablets.

Like many of the troops in the Pacific, Ishkode modified the kit to suit his own needs. Since he spent a lot of his time up in trees, where many biting insects resided, he used it to store extra bottles of the potent insect repellent the military doled out. He also took advantage of the fact that the kit was mostly waterproof, and stored extra bullets, a map, a pencil, and a candy bar—when he could get one—in the handy little pouch.

Although Ishkode's training included basic first aid, much of his knowledge was acquired from older tribal members back at the White Earth Indian Reservation—knowledge that had served both him and his sniping partners well, over time.

After tending Mata's leg, the two took off again and reached camp within two hours. The camp surgeon examined and dressed Mata's wound. "Good job with the first aid Trooper Redmond. This isn't serious but keep it wrapped and apply sulfa powder to it every eight hours. He should be up and around in a day or so."

Later in the day Captain Andersen poked at Ishkode. "You sure are hard on your spotters, Ishkode. We're going to start flying them in from the States just to keep up with you."

Ishkode laughed. "Sure seems so, Captain. But the corpsmen like me, because they get to try all their new stuff out. Maybe I'm in the wrong field."

"No, I think we'll keep you chained up around here. Do you want another assistant, or do you want to wait a day or two for that little guy?"

Ishkode considered the question. "You know, Captain, that damn Mata's a chowhound all the way, a nonstop chatterbox, and a pain in the rear...but he grows on you. I'd prefer to wait if that's okay."

Your call. Any idea when you'll go in?" Andersen asked.

"Give me two weeks, Captain. Then we'll get it done."

***

Major Hayate Iwata landed his autogyro at the cave containing the Japanese operational center on the island of Saipan. Iwata and his porter gathered their light gear and purposefully walked into the cave entrance, where two junior officers met them.

"Welcome, Major Iwata," the first said, bowing deeply. "Welcome, sir," the other repeated, following the first officer's lead, bowing deeply and keeping his eyes on the ground.

"This way to the control room, Major," the first officer straightened and gestured forward. "Colonel Niwa and Colonel Saito are waiting to greet you."

"Thank you," Iwata replied as he and his porter followed the men into the labyrinthine tunnels.

Major Iwata's visit had been anticipated by the Japanese hierarchy in Saipan with a degree of dread. The officers leading Iwata into the cave never imagined that Iwata was actually Ishkode Redmond, United States Marine. The Saipan native the Japanese officers saw as Iwata's porter was, in fact, Mata.

After the U.S. Navy broke the Japanese code in 1942, the Allies harvested information the Japanese forces transmitted as well as using that knowledge to spread disinformation to the Japanese. Operatives had transmitted information to the Saipan military forces regarding a visit to the island by Major Iwata, a supposedly important member of Emperor Hirohito's war cabinet. Expressing impatience with the progress on Saipan, the message informed command that the purpose of Iwata's visit was to find out why the Americans had not yet been driven off the island. Photos of "Major Iwata" were included with the communiqué. To

61

enhance the ruse, Ishkode had grown a thin mustache and donned a pair of clear round eyeglasses, similar to those worn by many Japanese officers. Ishkode also spent time learning some rudimentary Japanese words and phrases.

During training, Captain Andersen had said, "When the mission is complete, you'll be asked about the cave in detail, so get a good glimpse of everything. Their gun emplacements have effectively prevented the Air Corps and Navy from attacking the cave with aircraft, so any information you can provide about the cave's defensive weaponry will be of great service."

It took the group almost fifteen minutes to reach the inner sanctum of the cave where the main staff and hierarchy were located. As they walked through, Ishkode marveled at the natural fortress. At the front of the cave, elevated from the main entrance, were natural plateaus, which were ideal positions for heavy guns. Ishkode noted three separate emplacements, each with an artillery piece and two heavy machine guns.

The cave entrance itself was small and had a vault-like door to seal it off as needed. As they walked on through, they zigzagged through a tunnel system which itself had bulkhead type doors everyone hundred feet or so. When they finally entered the main cave, Ishkode was surprised to see natural light. It appeared that several shafts from the outer reaches of the cave were allowing light in, which the Japanese ingeniously enhanced with large well positioned mirrors.

"You are impressed with our little fortress, Major?" one of the escorts asked.

"Yes," Ishkode replied, after seeing Mata give him the high sign.

Ishkode wished he had enough mastery of the language to ask about their water supply, but the question answered itself as they passed several small streams of running water in various sections of the inner cavern.

When they reached an area of man-made rooms, they entered a large conference room with many charts and maps posted on the walls. Ishkode noted that the room appeared to have been built with soundproofing in mind.

"Please have a seat, Major," the escort offered while gesturing to a comfortable looking chair. "Colonel Niwa and Colonel Saito will be here soon." The officer poured Ishkode a cup of hot tea and ignored Mata.

Participation in many sniping missions had steeled Ishkode's nerves, so the pressure of walking around in the heart of the enemy control center did not fluster him. Mata, by nature, was not easily perturbed either. He even seemed a bit entertained, having worked there before, experiencing the same disdain from the Japanese. They barely glanced in his direction.

Mata still held out hope of shooting Ishkode's grease gun, which was hidden in the gear they'd brought in with them. "I shoot your gun today, maybe," he whispered after the escorts left the room.

"You just concentrate on releasing those smoke bombs when the time comes. Like I told you before, I do the shooting in this outfit," Ishkode reminded him.

Mata laid the three large map tubes they had brought on the table. Inside the tubes were the grease gun, five hand grenades, five smoke bombs, and a small machete. All would be employed to sow confusion after they assassinated their targets.

"Do you think you can remember the way back when it's time to get out of here?" Ishkode asked.

"Mata find way out easy…show you the way, master."

Before Ishkode could scold Mata for calling him master again, Colonel Niwa, Colonel Saito, and several junior officers entered the room. Ishkode leapt to his feet to salute the superior officers. Greetings were exchanged with a flurry of bowing, after which they all took seats for their discussion.

"You have new information for us, Major?" Colonel Saito bowed.

Ishkode gestured to Mata. The Japanese watched as the two removed the end caps from each tube. Mata clumsily knocked Ishkode's tea cup over, sending it to the floor with a crash. While the Japanese officers attention was diverted by the cup, Ishkode slid the grease gun and small machete out of one tube. Turning back in surprise, the Japanese jumped to their feet as Ishkode trained the gun on them and fired, hitting Niwa and Saito several times.

At the same time, Mata swiftly hacked two of the junior officers in the throat, causing them to scream out before they fell with blood gushing from their necks. The two remaining officers tried to flee toward the door, but Ishkode cut them down with the grease gun before they could get near it. He moved quickly to the colonels' bodies and shot each in the head.

Ishkode snapped another magazine into the grease gun and handed his Japanese service pistol to Mata. "Time to go!"

The two collected themselves, took a deep breath, and calmly walked out, closing the door behind them. Although the room had soundproofing, the shots had gotten the attention of nearby soldiers, who approached with caution. Without looking at anyone, Ishkode and Mata walked away from the room, heading back toward the exit tunnel. While some soldiers watched them, others went into the room and discovered the mayhem that had occurred. They ran out shouting and yelling, pointing at the two men who were now running toward the tunnel.

"Drop those smoke bombs!" Ishkode shouted.

Mata already had one in his hand. Pulling the igniting tab, he tossed it back and did the same with two more.

Black smoke filled the chamber, even as bullets started ricocheting off the stone walls of the cavern. Ishkode and Mata hustled out as quickly as possible, cautious not to take one of the many dead-end tunnels. They were fortunate that none of the heavy bulkhead doors had been locked and reached the main vault door at the cave entrance within ten minutes.

Ishkode stopped and raised his arm. "We better hold up and take a look. He slowly pushed the large door open enough to stick his head out. "Looks okay, the guards haven't been alerted yet. Let's go."

Taking another deep breath, the two men walked out of the cave toward their autogyro. As they reached the halfway point, a guard who was speaking on a two-way radio shouted at two others and pointed at Mata and Ishkode.

"Run!" Ishkode yelled.

The two took off, as all three enemy soldiers lifted their weapons and started firing. Ishkode made it another ten feet before he caught a bullet in his upper thigh. He tumbled like a gymnast before coming to a stop. Mata stopped to pick up his friend who struggled and regained his footing. Although his leg was badly damaged and bleeding profusely, Ishkode managed to get to the autogyro and climb in. Mata ignited the last smoke flare, creating a dense black fog. The three guards momentarily stopped shooting.

Below the cave entrance the supporting U.S. Marine contingent took the commotion as their cue and started firing a heavy machine gun and small artillery piece at the surface of the mountain several hundred feet above the cave entrance. The Japanese machine gun nests near the entrance returned fire, even though they had no good target.

By the time Ishkode cranked up the autogyro, the smoke had blown clear. The three guards, who took up positions behind large rocks when the Marines started shooting, had a clear line of fire to the autogyro.

"Get in!" Ishkode screamed.

Mata, who'd been exchanging fire with the guards

while the autogyro cranked up, turned and climbed in. The gyro lifted and pulled away as the guards continued to fire. Ishkode turned just in time to see Mata jerk as one of the high caliber rounds pierced his back.

"Hang on, Mata!"

The autogyro gained altitude, coming under more intense fire until the fuselage was shredded with holes. The small craft faltered and lost altitude. As it rapidly approached the ground below the cave entrance—and the relative safety of the Marine contingent—Ishkode managed to keep it horizontal. It struck the ground with jarring force. Not having been strapped in, Ishkode hit the windshield and roof, immediately losing consciousness.

***

After receiving medical attention at the camp, Ishkode was taken to a U.S. naval field hospital. Captain Andersen arrived almost before Ishkode got there.

"How are you, Ishkode?"

Sedated and disoriented, Ishkode whispered. "I'm kind of groggy, sir. Where are we?"

"At a field hospital. They've stabilized you and will be taking you to surgery to take care of that leg."

"We got em, Captain." Ishkode mouthed quietly.

Andersen grasped Ishkode's hand. "You did, Ishkode! You and Mata provided a service to your country for which the Marines and all of America are grateful."

Ishkode raised himself and looked around. "Mata?"

"We'll talk about him when you get out of surgery."

***

Several days later Ishkode woke up to see Captain Andersen sitting beside his bed.

"Captain! Didn't think I'd see you here again."

"I wanted to see you before they shipped you home, Ishkode."

Ishkode looked hopefully at Andersen. "Have you seen Mata? When can I visit him? Where is he?"

The captain clenched his jaw before continuing. "He didn't make it, Ishkode. The bullet pierced his spinal column. He'll be buried here, with full military honors."

Ishkode remained quiet. Though he maintained an outward stoicism, he was still deeply affected by the deaths of his friends. He still hadn't really gotten over the death of Harold Karsten. And now this.

"You okay, Ishkode?" Captain Andersen asked.

Ishkode took a minute to answer. "I'll be okay...I guess the good really do die young, as they say."

"You know, they also say that as long as people remain in our hearts and in our minds, they're still with us. I believe Mata—and Harold—will remain with us for the rest of our lives."

"Thank you, Captain. I think they will."

Andersen took a long pause, "Ishkode...the surgeon had to remove your leg."

Ishkode nodded. "I knew that, Captain. The doctors thought they fooled me, but I knew they took it off. I'll deal with it."

The captain hoped to sound encouraging. "I'm told they're developing prosthetic legs, which will enable you to stand and walk...at some point in the future."

"But I can still stay in the Marines. Right?"

Andersen had a tough time with this question and took a deep breath.

"You'll always be a Marine, Ishkode. But the Marines have no facilities or the capability to provide for those that are disabled. The war is over for you. You'll receive a pension and lifetime healthcare benefits. Local industries in your home state that provide employment for disabled veterans will be forwarded your information."

"I don't believe there are any of those on our reservation back in Minnesota, Captain." Ishkode said quietly.

Andersen nodded. "I'm sure you're right. You'll have to make many adjustments to your life. You can do it... you're a Marine. For your actions you will be awarded the Silver Star and possibly the Navy Cross. I know that doesn't get your leg back, and I also want you to know I am your friend Ishkode...I will always be your friend."

CHAPTER 9

L t. Col. Montrell busied himself with preparations for the next raids on Japan, scheduled to take place in August.

The Yawata bombing mission in June had not been successful regarding damage inflicted on the Japanese homeland. But the attack laid the foundation for future raids that would cripple Japan's ability to continue the fight. It also demoralized the citizenry of Japan, and dampened any hope of Japan winning the war. Many weaknesses in Japan's air defenses were exposed. However, five B-29s were lost to accidents, and two were shot down by Japanese fighters.

Two weeks after the Yawata mission, members of the B-29 wing at Chengtu conducted a formal memorial for Sergeant Richard Williams and the other fifty-seven men who were killed in the raid.

Montrell set up a commander's call in the hangar to address the men soon after. He now looked around at his gathered command. "We're relocating, men. The raid on Yawata was just a taste of what's in store for Japan. However, from a practical standpoint, we need to move our base of operations closer to our targets. As we speak, Marines, soldiers, Air Corps personnel, and sailors are fighting in the Mariana Islands to expel the Japanese from their foothold there. Once they are removed, B-29s will be stationed there to pound the Japanese homeland nonstop. We'll be operating day and night. I expect this information to stay within this group. We'll spend the next couple of months studying maps, performing maintenance and bombing drills, and preparing for the move. We also expect to take on additional missions as the need arises. If you have any questions, bring them to your immediate NCOIC or OIC. In the Navy they say loose lips sink ships. Well, here in the Air Corps, we don't lose our lips. Dismissed!"

The airmen laughed at the colonel's joke as they left the hangar.

Montrell called for an additional meeting at base operations to be attended by all officers of his flight at 0800 hours the next morning. However, that evening, Montrell received orders to report to the office of Brigadier General Kenneth Wolfe at 0700 hours the next morning. Upon inquiry, Montrell was told he need not cancel his flight officers' meeting that was scheduled an hour later.

Wolfe and Montrell had served together in the Canadian Air Force before the United States got involved in World War II. They both moved on as flight instructors when the United States jumped into the war. Wolfe, however, got a combat assignment early, making bombing runs over Germany while flying out of England. When Wolfe got orders to the Pacific to head up the B-29 effort there, he specifically asked for Raymond Montrell to be in his wing. Now they were both poised to take the war to the Japanese homeland and bring the Japs to their knees.

Montrell reported to General Wolfe the next morning as ordered.

"I don't remember how you take your coffee, Ray," General Wolfe said as he poured from a fresh carafe.

"Well, usually black with a shot of brandy, Ken." Montrell reminded him.

Laughing, General Wolfe now recalled those days, "Oh yeah, we did throw a few of those down with the Canucks,

didn't we? We'll have to do without the brandy this morning, but we sure won't at the club later on tonight. And we
have good reason for a few toasts." Wolfe handed Montrell
two silver eagles representing the rank of full bird colonel.
"I'm bumping you up, Ray. That way you can afford to buy
a few rounds when we're there."

Surprised, Montrell held the two silver birds in his
hand for a moment. "Thank you...thank you, Ken."

"You might not thank me after you find out how much
work I've got in store for you. I'm handing the Saipan
operation over to you. It'll be up to you to be the Air Corps
man to bird-dog the effort to get rid of the Japs and to lay
out the schedule to get the B-29s in there. We're gonna
bomb the piss out of Japan from Saipan once we kick their
Jap asses off the island."

The general's words intrigued Montrell. "Will I be
involved in the layout of the base as well?"

Wolfe nodded. "You'll put together the team that takes
care of the whole enchilada. I have every confidence in
you, Ray. Oh, by the way, did I mention you will also be
responsible for training as well as bombing missions in
Indochina and the Philippines in the meantime?"

"Will I be working with you?" Montrell asked.

"Not as much as I'd like. There's a big project coming
and the B-29 will have a major stake. It's top secret so I
can't say any more about it. But it looks like it'll be keeping me busy for the foreseeable future."

"Well, good luck with that, sir."

"Thanks, Ray, and to you as well. Now pin on those
birds and let your boys see 'em at this morning's meeting.
If you're available tonight, let's have that shot of brandy."

At Colonel Montrell's eight o'clock officers' meeting, he
brought them all up to speed on new events involving the
wing—as much as he was able to divulge. A popular leader,
Montrell's promotion in rank and status was well received
by his men.

Within hours of the meeting, Montrell received another call from the wing commander. A target of opportunity had developed. A Japanese battleship group that survived Midway and other encounters was steaming back to Japan. The B-29 wing in China was being tasked with laying mines in shallow harbors up and down the Japanese seaboard, in an attempt to destroy the incoming flotilla. The mission had risks, as the task required the B-29s to fly at low altitude. They would be subjected to the anti-aircraft defense shield along with the defensive barrage balloons and low-flying Japanese Zeros.

"Looks like we'll have to have that drink another time, Ray."

"No problem, sir. Nailing that battle group will be a significant loss to the Japs. I look forward to that."

"Damn straight," Wolfe agreed. "And there's a good chance those mines will put a hurt on all the oil barges supplying Japan as well. Good luck, Ray."

The rest of the day and most of the week involved fitting up the B-29 bomb bays with equipment suited to carry the mines.

The huge bombers also needed a change in weaponry. Montrell's B-29 was not the only one to have rear gun problems during the Yawata raid.

They tested and retested the guns throughout the week. Crews made low-level test runs around the clock, with the B-29s doing stop-and-goes steadily for days. As always, fuel ran short, and command tasked Montrell with the responsibility of ensuring there were sufficient reserves at all B-29 bases in China. He informed the air crews that they would be flying every day for at least a month, until the mission was complete.

Another problem they had to address was engine reliability. The four Wright R-3350, eighteen-cylinder engines powering the B-29s experienced high failure rates and spare parts were constantly being expedited in from the

States. Of the five test days leading up to the mining raid, crews reported seventy-nine instances of engine failure. This news concerned Montrell.

In a heated meeting with the head of aircraft maintenance, Montrell lost patience. "I don't want to lose ten percent of our fleet to mechanical failure like we did in Yawata."

"Those engines were untested. We can't be held accountable for aircraft we haven't gone over, sir," Major Norbert Morton objected.

"I don't want any goddamn excuses, Morton. You make sure those engines are run up on the ground before the birds lift off."

"And how will I do that if the birds aren't in maintenance long enough for the run up, sir?"

Montrell was exasperated. "Why aren't these engines vetted out before they're sent here?"

"Colonel, we've been asking that for months, ever since the days back in India. We've even offered to fly men back to the depots to perform the maintenance run outs ourselves. But we get no response."

"I know you've been doing your best, Norb. It's just frustrating to lose air crews and aircraft for lack of maintenance."

"I agree one-hundred percent, sir. And we intend to work around the clock to see that it doesn't happen."

"Well if you need any help, we can cross-train gunners, clerks, or cooks to jump in."

"Colonel, you send me thirty of the nastiest men you've got and we'll turn them into grease monkeys within the week," Morton promised

***

Montrell's flight completed seven missions, dropping mines in harbors up and down the Japanese coast in the following weeks. The deployed mines destroyed many enemy vessels and damaged even more, contributing to the growing success of the Allied effort in the Pacific.

Maintenance had made good on their promise to improve the performance of the B-29 engines. Several B-29s were damaged by anti-aircraft fire, but the losses were rapidly decreasing.

"Fine job, Ray. Those mines put a hurt on Japan. They can't move material in or out. I'm sorry for your losses, but glad they're lower than before."

"Thanks, General. Credit goes to all the crews, both air and ground. And it looks like Saipan is just about clear of Japs. If it weren't for the Marine and Army grunts doing such a great job, we wouldn't be able to use Saipan for attacking mainland Japan. I heard it was brutal. Japs hiding out in caves, ravines, whatever. God knows how many of our guys died. And the rest will be having nightmares for a long time to come."

"Yeah, as bad as it can be in the air, I'd rather be flying than down in a foxhole somewhere."

"The Seabees have started on the runways already."

Wolfe nodded. "Thank God for those Seabees. Have your crews been learning from them?"

"Yes, sir. They love the Seabees. The Navy recruited actual construction workers, so they really are skilled. And they know what they're doing. But our crews are still a little pissed off that the Navy has to come in and build our bases for us. Some day that will change."

Wolfe winked. "Don't think there's enough time left in this war...maybe the next one, Ray."

PART TWO

The end of one war sows the seeds of another.

THE KOREAN WAR

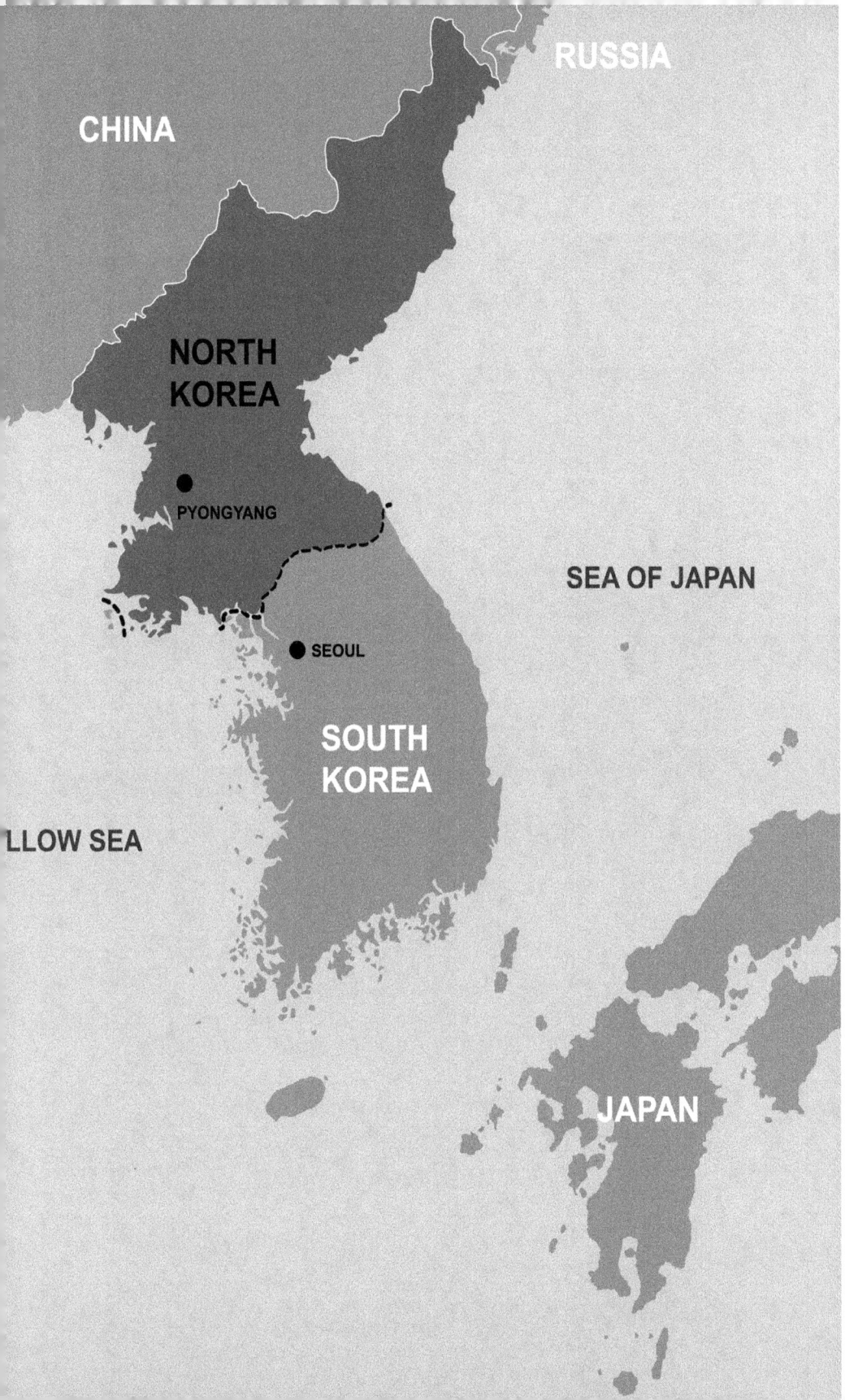

CHAPTER 10

"Bomb bay doors open," Colonel Montrell ordered.

"Bomb bay doors open," the bombardier repeated.

"Execute bombing procedure," Montrell ordered.

The squadron of fifteen B-29s under Montrell's command all released their 260-pound fragmentation bombs over the target area, which was believed to contain the bulk of North Korean troops that had attacked South Korea.

Five days earlier, the North Korean People's Army (NKPA), had invaded the South. Unprepared for such aggression, the United States scrambled to come to the aid of the South Koreans. After all that had occurred, they felt responsible for the fledgling nation.

Before World War II, the Korean peninsula was part of the Japanese empire. After the war, the land was divided across the middle, at the 38th Parallel. The Soviets protected the land north of the line and the Americans protected the south.

President Truman had gone on record saying, "If we let Korea down, the Soviets will keep right on going and swallow up one after another." The newly formed United States Air Force was in the process of making sure that didn't happen.

Montrell had warned the senior command that the B-29s, while appropriate for strategic bombing missions, might have limited success in a tactical role. And as Montrell feared, the bombing run proved to do little damage to the invaders, who had moved out of the target area days before. "Well, we had to take a shot at it," Brigadier General George Stratemeyer remarked at the mission debriefing at Kadena Airbase, Okinawa. "You were right, Montrell. You may now execute your plan to begin the strategic bombing in the north. I'll grease the skids with command."

Montrell had mapped an operation to take out bridges, roads, bases, and factories in the northern half of the peninsula, a job much better suited to the high-flying B-29s. The bombs would have delayed-action fuses so they could not be disarmed, as many of the bombs in the earlier mission had been.

Montrell's central fire control gunner from World War II, Marvin Dobbs, now a major, had joined his staff as the B-29 defensive weapons coordinator. Henry Bohn, Montrell's former copilot, was now a lieutenant colonel. And although Montrell had commanded the anti-personnel bombing mission on June 30, Bohn was now the senior flight commander and would call signals for all future missions.

"When will we launch the campaign, Ray?" Bohn inquired.

"We're starting next week. I'm counting on General Stratemeyer to have the plan approved by then."

"Will you be in the flight?" Bohn hadn't objected when Montrell took command of the earlier bombing mission, but he did want to know when his role as flight leader would begin in full. "You have a new baby at home, now...I wouldn't blame you if you sat this one out." Bohn added.

"Yeah, little Douglas is just learning to walk and jabber." Montrell understood Bohn's concern. "I'm going along, Hank. But I won't be nosing around in your bailiwick on this trip. I'm going to be sitting with the gunny and the flight engineer. We want to make sure those engines and guns hold up, because we can expect a significant amount of ack-ack over the target area. If the revisions haven't corrected the problems we've had, I'm personally flying back to Boeing to kick ass and take names."

Bohn was fine with that. "Yes sir, Colonel. We need the guns and the damn engines to hold up much better than they have so far. Might as well go back to the B-24s if these don't prove out."

***

Lieutenant Colonel Bohn's flight of seventeen B-29s dropped their payload of general-purpose bombs over the bridges, railways, and other strategic elements of the North Korean city of Pyongyang. Although incendiary firebombs would have been more effective, President Truman refused to allow them because of the massive negative feedback after World War II.

Unlike the previous mission that targeted North Korean troops, this mission was highly successful. Each aircraft released all forty of their five-hundred-pound bombs, destroying or seriously damaging many North Korean objectives.

The flight was harassed by a minimal amount of anti-aircraft fire, and it was well below the altitude of the B-29s. Three North Korean aircraft met them in a futile attempt to threaten the large bombers but were quickly destroyed by withering fire from the B-29 gun turrets.

"Very good mission, Hank," Montrell was content as the flight returned to their base in Okinawa. He was situated next to the flight engineer, where he'd been monitoring the status of the defensive guns as well as the engines. "Thanks, Colonel. And it sure looks like those fixes to the engines and guns have paid off."

"Thank God, even though only two birds had a chance to use their guns, they sure did the job. Have you heard from the spotter?"

The spotter was the designated B-29 assigned to fly low over the target area after the mission. He made visual observations and took pictures to assess the effectiveness of the bombing.

"He reported all targets hit and damaged," Bohn replied. "Apparently his camera had some problems, but we'll take a look back at base ops. Will you hold the debriefing, sir?"

"I will. There's been talk of a heavy influx of war materiel from China. Intel says it appears to be new anti-aircraft weapons as well as Russian MiGs. We may have to compress our bombing runs, to create as much damage as we can before their new weapons are up and running."

***

"We'll have to go with fighter escorts on all of our runs. It's the only way," Brigadier General Stratemeyer informed his wing commanders in Okinawa. After the first few missions, the North Koreans responded as predicted with advanced anti-aircraft guns and MiG-15s provided by the Soviet Union and China. To date, fourteen B-29s had been shot down, with the loss of the complete air crew in each case.

"General, I have some concerns." Montrell wasn't comfortable with this latest plan. "On occasion, we've waited up to five hours for our fighter jets to show up, and in some cases, they didn't show at all. I hate to see our missions stall to the point where the North Korean ability to wage war is not adversely affected by our bombing."

Stratemeyer felt there was no other choice. "I agree, Ray. But I'm firm on this, if we can't provide fighter escort, we'll try to reach the strategic areas with our battleship groups off the coast. We can't lose the B-29s at our current rate and still remain a viable force."

Montrell hoped for a better choice. "Sir, we could attempt more night missions. We've been getting better at it."

"We'll have to discuss that further, Ray. The North Koreans have been timing their ack-ack in order to take our bombers down, even at night. But there may be a way to alter our bombing patterns to lessen the enemy's effectiveness. I've got to attend a coalition briefing in thirty minutes. Let's get together tomorrow morning at 0800 hours. We'll meet in the big hangar. Have all the air crews attend, and we'll pick their brains as well."

"Yes, sir," Montrell replied.

CHAPTER 11

With the South Korean Army being pushed toward the sea at the southernmost point of the peninsula, the United States threw everything they had available at the North Koreans in an attempt to slow them down.

The B-29s had proved to be of poor use in tactical warfare, and their attempt to stem the North Korean advance did not accomplish its goal. The 1st Marine Division had been ordered to mobilize. But having been drawn down from its World War II levels, it needed time to re-man and get underway—time the South Koreans didn't have.

The 5th Marine Regiment was cobbled together with 4,700 available troops in the Pacific. Supported by Marine Aircraft Group 33, the 5th Marine Regiment landed at Pusan on August 3, 1950, and was immediately thrown at the advancing North Korean Army.

***

"Hold 'em! Hold 'em!" Marine Captain Ike Fenton screamed.

North Korean reinforcements were making a counteroffensive after Fenton and B Company of the 5th Marine Regiment pushed the North Koreans off the Obong-ni Ridge.

Lance Corporal Chibenashi Redmond manned the .50 caliber heavy machine gun, since both the original gunner and his replacement had been killed. Bird, as Chibenashi was sometimes called, mowed down the advancing North Korean troops like wheat. Private Jim Ortiz fed belts of .50 caliber bullets into the machine gun, while Chibenashi lashed out with the lethal weapon.

"Seven belts left!" Ortiz shouted.

"We'll pull back when we're out," Chibenashi told him. "Scream when you hand me the last one."

"I'm screaming already, buddy. When we're down to one, I'll crap my pants."

With the whole company low on ammunition, Fenton ordered everyone back to a defensible position before they completely ran out. The North Koreans, sensing an opportunity, launched another attack. At least three hundred of them jumped up and charged B Company's position all at once. However, as the Koreans reached mid-point in their charge, fifteen U.S. Marine F4U Corsairs roared in and decimated the attacking troops. The Corsairs made run after run until there were fewer than fifty North Koreans left.

Bird and Ortiz picked up the M1 Garands off their dead comrades, and with other survivors from their company, slaughtered the remaining North Koreans. The Marines then regrouped and marched to their staging area, where they would get resupplied.

"Get any mail, Bird?" Ortiz asked. The two close friends always kept each other informed about their families and home life.

"Letter from Ma."

"How's your brother?"

Chibenashi didn't hear much about that in the letter. "She didn't say much about him, so I'm guessing nothing's changed."

Chibenashi worshipped his older brother Ishkode and had joined the Marine Corps in his honor, though Ishkode didn't acknowledge the act. After losing his leg in World War II, Ishkode had returned to the reservation in Northern Minnesota, where he spent his days drinking until he passed out. He'd been hospitalized on and off with various infections in his leg, as well as acute alcoholism. Although he never received a reply, Chibenashi wrote to him every week.

***

Two days later, Chibenashi and Jim sat quietly in their position. The 5th Marine Regiment had advanced fifty miles, chasing the North Koreans, who stopped on occasion to skirmish in an attempt to slow their pursuers down.

Jim Ortiz looked through the squad's small spotting scope. "What the hell?"

"What's up, Jim? Are they surrendering or has General MacArthur arrived?" Bird quipped.

"Better yet. It's our old buddy, Two Toes."

Chibenashi grabbed the scope and peered through it. "I don't fucking believe it." There, limping along in a ragged old uniform with no helmet was the same man they'd previously identified as Two Toes. "Yep, it's him. Still has the uniform with the black burn marks on it, and he hasn't found his damn helmet yet."

Though not as well equipped as the NATO troops, the North Koreans fought ferociously. In many of the engagements, they were all left dead on the field. Surrender and retreat apparently were not in their vocabulary.

When their company was pinned down by North Korean skirmishers the week before, they'd watched as deadly fire from the Corsairs wreaked havoc among the invading troops. While in pursuit, Ortiz found a boot with part of a foot inside, including three toes. Incredibly, the boot owner limped away with the rest of his unit, evidenced by his odd footprints in the soft dirt. Bird and Ortiz occasionally saw the half-boot print among skirmishers they were pursuing.

"That bastard has got to be the toughest sonofabitch in the North Korean army," Bird remarked.

"Toughest sonofabitch in any army," Ortiz countered. "You'd think the little bastard would've died of blood poisoning by now."

Bird shook his head and took aim with his M1 Garand. "I'm gonna put him out of his misery, once and for all."

After Chibenashi squeezed off five shots, Ortiz looked through the scope again. "Nothing there," he observed.

"Fucker's got more lives than a damn cat." Chibenashi grumbled.

"Are you two still wasting bullets on that cripple?" Captain Fenton asked as he walked over. "Time to form up. We're heading back to the last base camp for another mission.

"C'mon, Captain, give us one more day. I'm gonna get the rest of those toes and shove 'em where the sun don't shine," Ortiz protested.

"I can't believe you haven't put him down yet. You're one of the best shots in the entire Marine Corps," Fenton noted.

"Hell, I think he's just a spirit, anyway," Bird was a bit perplexed.

"Spirit, my ass," Fenton shot back. "He's just got a couple of rookies plinking at him. Might be we need to get those dogface army bastards up here to shoot that three-toed bastard."

"Two-toed." Ortiz corrected. "And I'll out-shoot any Army grunt they send up here...sir."

"Well, we don't have time to find out," Fenton laughed. "Form up, and let's point it south."

***

As the North Korean People's Army launched massive counterattacks, the stalwart Marines bent but did not break. Captain Fenton's company took a terrible beating.

They had started out with one hundred and fifty men. In fighting up to this point they had taken fifteen killed in action and twenty-seven wounded. Fenton had requested replacements twice, but none had arrived as of yet.

"You two dead-eyes shamed third platoon again. Well done," Fenton remarked.

Chibenashi Redmond and Jim Ortiz stood at attention as Captain Ike Fenton pinned Purple Heart Medals on each of them, as well as several others who had been wounded during the sieges the Marines had been subjected to for the past few weeks. At the same ceremony, Redmond and Ortiz were both promoted—Chibenashi to sergeant and Jim to lance corporal.

After the short ceremony, Bird and Ortiz returned to their post, which they had held through bitter fighting. Chibenashi nursed a shoulder wound, while Ortiz limped as a result of a bullet wound to his left calf. Fenton was badly wounded in the thigh and could barely walk. He still managed to carry on and maintain his chipper demeanor.

"Do you think they'll send him home?" Ortiz wondered. Chibenashi doubted that would happen. "We're undermanned, they can't, and as Ike himself always says 'If they send everyone home with a mosquito bite, we might as well surrender.'"

"Don't know how many more mosquito bites Ike can take," Ortiz noted. "And hey, if you know a tailor, we can get these new stripes sewed on. Then maybe we'll get invited to the officer's mess."

Chibenashi laughed. "Hell, get out that damn sewing kit they issued you in boot camp, Lance Corporal Ortiz. You can practice on yours and then sew my sergeant's stripes after you get the hang of it."

Ortiz didn't get a chance to answer, as intense rifle fire erupted from the woods where North Korean troops had been massing.

"Fuck!" Ortiz shouted, while feeding belts of ammunition into the .50 caliber machine gun for Chibenashi. Dozens of NKPA troops who had charged out of the woods fell like wheat to the sickle as the heavy machine gun spit out lead.

"Fuck you, assholes!" Chibenashi shouted as he continued to mow down the charging riflemen.

Suddenly his gun stopped firing and he realized he was out of ammunition. "Get that belt loaded!" he screamed, turning toward Ortiz. "Those fuckers will be in our laps in a minute..."

Chibenashi looked at his new lance corporal, realizing why Ortiz no longer fed him belts of ammunition as a large exit wound in the back of his friend's head gushed blood. Redmond was snapped out of his stupor when Captain Fenton jumped into the hide, pushed Ortiz's body aside, and started feeding belts of ammo into the .50 cal.

"Fire that goddamn thing, Bird, or I'll shoot you myself." Fenton yelled.

Chibenashi mumbled but resumed fire at the charging troops, whose numbers were being greatly reduced by Marine machine gun and mortar teams. As the enemy reached the American positions, they attacked viciously with rifle butts and bayonets. When the .50 Cal was no longer effective on the scattered incoming North Koreans, Fenton used his .45 caliber pistol, killing five or six who reached their emplacement.

Chibenashi shot several with his M1 Garand and disposed of several more with his bayonet.

Depleted of troops, the charge ended. A dozen or more North Koreans retreated to the woods from which they came. Many were shot retreating, as the Marines' heavy machine guns came to life once again. When the firefight was over, Chibenashi picked up his friend's body and held him for several minutes.

CHAPTER 12

AUGUST 1950

PUSAN, SOUTH KOREA

U.S. ARMY 25TH INFANTRY DIVISION

U.S. Army Major Jack Tobin implored his men. "We're moving them back, men, just keep the pressure on. We'll kick them back over that border pretty damn quick."

A company commander in the 25th Infantry Division, Tobin and his men had been engaged with the North Koreans since they deployed from Hawaii to Pusan in July, a month prior. The Koreans had made counterattack after counterattack, but the weary men of the 25th seemed to be gaining ground in the battle.

Private First-Class Mario Crucianelli, a member of 1st Platoon, Company B, moved up with the rest of the men.

"Got any cigarettes, Mario?" Private Gustav Dietz asked.

"Damn, Gus, you must've gone through the whole platoon's ration of smokes by now. Why don't you send for some of those Kraut cigarettes, anyway?"

"I am a damn U.S. citizen, you know. I don't have to smoke that German shit anymore," he grumbled.

Gustav was a former World War II German prisoner of war. After being interned in Wisconsin, he was released into a farming community near the POW camp. He went to work for a farmer who thought he had struck gold, for Gus was the "hardest working sonofabitch" he had on his dairy farm.

"Just what did you do besides milking cows and pestering the farmer's wife when you were a prisoner?" Mario wanted to know.

"I am a gentleman, I pestered no one. Besides, I was the only German in my unit who could speak English, so they made me a supervisor."

Laughing, Mario shook his head. "The fox in the henhouse!"

Dietz scoffed. "I was treated better as a prisoner of war than in that dummkopf's army."

Mario was still laughing. "Are you referring to der Führer?"

"He ruined Germany, that two-bit Bohemian jackass corporal...him and your Italian buddy Mussolini."

"You got that right. Mussolini sure ruined Italy, he was a real horses ass. But just what did you do on the farm, anyway?"

Dietz was proud of his farm work. "I helped build a barn. You know I was a carpenter back home, so that's what I did in Wisconsin."

Mario prodded the German a bit. "I would have thought you shoveled shit."

"I only do that after you speak," Dietz fired back.

Mario doubled over laughing. "So how'd you end up in the American army, anyway?"

Dietz's expression changed. "One Saturday night the American guards took us to town. We had no demerits all month, so they allowed us a night on our own. We went into a lovely little tavern to have some beer. But the damn bartender wouldn't let us in."

"Didn't want any Nazis in his place, huh?"

"You Americans are good people, but you sometimes shame yourselves. One of our guards was a Negro. The bartender wouldn't allow him in the tavern."

"Damn, is that when the shit hit the fan?"

Dietz nodded. "The bartender grabbed a truncheon and tried to beat the man because he refused to leave. I was closest, so I grabbed the truncheon out of his hands and held onto him so he couldn't move. Soon the police came and arrested our whole damn bunch. The next morning, they turned us over to the prison guards, who threw me and the Negro guard in jail."

"Did you get a hearing?"

"Damn right we did. The judge was a very fair man. He apologized to the Negro for the actions of the white men at the bar, and for getting thrown in the stockade."

"Good man. But what's that got to do with you joining the army?" Mario wanted to know.

"The judge told everyone in the court that, even though I was a German POW and former enemy, I was the only one who showed the real spirit of America that night. He dismissed the charge of assault and told me if I wanted to leave prison, he had the power to release me, if I agreed to join the United States military."

"So here you are, Gus!" Mario now understood.

"Here I am, smoking all the platoon's cigarettes."

Mario contemplated his own journey to this place. It seemed like yesterday that the Western Union messenger had showed up on their porch. Seeing him coming up the stone sidewalk, Mario's mother turned her back and froze, hoping against hope that the news would not be delivered. His sister Eleanor answered the door and accepted the telegram, informing them of the death of Dante Crucianelli.

Mario was devastated. Though too young to join the military, he intended to sign up in 1946, as soon as he turned eighteen. On his birthday, his mother Nicolina beseeched him not to go.

"I have already lost my firstborn to war," she lamented. "I will not stand by and bury another son because some idiot has decided the world needs another one."

"There's no war going on, Mama. I'll spend two years in the Army and learn a good trade for when I get out."

"There will soon be a war, Mario." Although Nicolina had no formal education, she had a keen mind and could read and write. She followed the news and kept up with current events. "There is always a war somewhere. And since America survived the last war with less damage than other countries, we have now become the policeman of the world. The communists are stirring the pot, and it won't be long before fighting breaks out."

Frustrated but not wanting to put his mother through any more pain, Mario bided his time. Ever since Korea had been divided in May of 1945, the winds of war were churning. President Truman, on advice from frantic military leaders, signed the Selective Service Act of 1948, requiring all men between the ages of eighteen and twenty-six to register. This was the opening Mario had been waiting for. "If there is going to be a war, I want to be ready and properly trained for it," he told his mother. "If I join now, I'll have a better chance of doing that than if I get drafted after a war breaks out."

With the handwriting on the wall, Nicolina reluctantly gave in. Mario Crucianelli joined the U.S. Army the day after his twentieth birthday.

***

Back at camp, Major Tobin addressed his men.

"Listen up, men. We have a new mission. The 5th Marines are moving back. They've got a new assignment and we have to cover their damn asses again."

Major Tobin's remark brought a round of laughter from his infantry company, who had been aggressively pushing a large North Korean unit back toward the DMZ.

"We're going to slide over and chase the rest of those commie bastards back to their stinking dirt holes up north. They've slowed the Marines down with skirmishing squads and hurt their feelings. The Army will take care of it for them."

The men formed up in columns and marched the rest of the day, until they bivouacked at around 1800 hours. As always, PFCs Gustav Dietz and Mario Crucianelli shared a tent.

"Why do you suppose the jarheads bugged out?" Mario wondered.

Dietz shrugged. "Hell, there is no glory to be had chasing five or six gooks around. Those Marines are used to a big blow so they can pin a few more medals on their chests. Let the Army clean up the messy stuff."

Mario got a kick out of Dietz's rant. "Give 'em hell, Gus. You gonna eat them beans?"

"I ate enough goddamn beans back in Visconsin to float a battleship. You can finish 'em."

In the morning, the company formed up and Major Tobin briefed them. "Groups of up to ten North Koreans have been floating back and forth, attacking the Marine companies chasing them. Our orders are to push them back over the DMZ and take as many prisoners as we can. The Marines are getting nickel and dimed with casualties because of these goddamn skirmishing patrols. I don't intend to take the same casualties. As far as I'm concerned, a dead gook is better than a prisoner. Tomorrow morning, we move out in squads, cleaning up these skirmishers until we run into the main North Korean force which is retreating. It is not my intention to take prisoners at any point in this campaign. If my meaning is unclear, speak up."

***

"These skirminchers are a pain in the ass," Dietz complained.

"Skirmishers, buddy. And you fucking Krauts did the same thing to us when we chased you from France to Berlin."

"I skirminched nobody, I fought your damn parachute men in France.

Mario wouldn't leave it alone. "Yeah, and where did that get you, Gus?"

"It got me to Visconsin, where I had all the cheese I could crap."

"And it got you on this nice all-expenses-paid vacation to the Far East."

"And stuck in a tent with one of Mussolini's poorer relatives."

The two bantered until breaking camp with the rest of the company and pushing forward again. The unit continued to engage in firefights with the NKPA skirmishers who had previously hounded the Marines. But the 25th Infantry patiently worked its way up the peninsula, cleaning out nests of North Korean invaders as they went.

Mario was looking at the ground curiously. "Take a look at this."

Dietz moved closer. Along with the normal boot prints in the soft dirt, there were prints of what seemed to be a one-legged man trailing along with the others—a full boot print accompanied by a round imprint.

"Peg-Leg Pete!"

"Those fucking North Koreans are so bad off, they're recruiting cripples and invalids," Mario said. "The next thing you know, gooks in wheelchairs will be shooting at us."

"Well, if they can't shoot any better than you, that'd be fine with me."

Dietz was not far off the mark. Though a stalwart trooper and tough campaigner, Mario Crucianelli was possibly the worst shot in the infantry. Major Tobin had finally given up on him and replaced his M1 with a Remington 12-gauge pump action shotgun. Loaded with double aught shot, Mario became proficient with it...as long as he was within range.

"Hey, I can nail anything within thirty yards," Mario protested.

"I'll ask the major to have the gooks come stand in front of you, so you can shoot them," Dietz said. "Maybe you can hit these cripples they're sending out now."

"You didn't bitch when I shot the one that was sneaking up on you the other day."

"He wouldn't have got me. I think he was one of the blind ones."

"Next time I'll let one shoot you, so I don't have to listen to you bitch all the time."

"Then I'd get a nice bed in the hospital ship where the nurses would give me massages every day."

"The only thing they'd massage is that bald head of yours. How come all you Krauts go bald at the age of ten, anyway?"

Dietz scoffed. "We have big brains, they outgrow our hair. You dagos with the black forest on your heads don't have that problem."

"Will you two shut the fuck up and look for sign?" Major Tobin interrupted. "I might as well have a damn troop of Cub Scouts out here."

"Cub Scouts get hot food and a warm bed at night," Dietz pointed out.

"So do jailbirds and fucking POWs," the major replied as Mario doubled over in laughter. "And if you don't shut your trap, you'll end up back there."

CHAPTER 13

CHONGJIN, NORTH KOREA
U.S. AIR FORCE 19TH BOMBARDMENT WING

Lieutenant Colonel Henry Bohn moved his flight of B-29s into holding pattern thirty-thousand feet above Chongjin. This night mission would be the first to implement the new bombing pattern hammered out by the 19th Bombardment Wing back in Okinawa.

"Aircrafts 113, 117, and 121 proceed," Bohn ordered.

The three B-29s, loaded with twenty-thousand pounds of general-purpose bombs, swept into their individual bombing patterns and dropped their ordinance on predetermined targets. In exactly three minutes, three more bombers left the flight and headed for their predetermined altitude and target areas, releasing their payloads over their designated spots. The rest of the flight followed the plan as well, with all aircraft successfully releasing their payloads on target.

The B-29s swept in from the west and departed over the Sea of Japan. As the bombing raid progressed, furious anti-aircraft fire broke out over the city. In addition to the anti-aircraft fire, ten MiG-15s were sent up to challenge the bombers. The new swept-back Russian jets were much faster than previous aircraft and provided a serious challenge to the lumbering B-29s. Almost all seventeen bombers in the flight were hit with shrapnel from the anti-aircraft fire as well. One of them took three large hits to the fuselage.

Flying behind the distressed aircraft, Bohn watched helplessly as it spun out of control and crashed.

"Anyone see any chutes?" he asked.

No one had seen any parachutes from the downed aircraft, and they had little time to look for any as they themselves were now taking fire from the MiGs which were swarming around them like angry wasps.

"I thought those fuckers couldn't fly at night," the weapons engineer yelled to no one in particular, while directing furious return fire at the MiGs.

"They've got some type of new radar system which supposedly allows them to navigate better at night," Bohn answered. "Let's get the hell out of here before we're all splashed."

*****

General Stratemeyer, Colonel Montrell, and Lieutenant Colonel Bohn met in Okinawa the day after the raid on Chongjin.

Stratemeyer was pleased. "Eighty-five percent of strategic targets hit, with fifty percent destroyed completely. Those new bombing patterns did the job."

"Yes, sir," Montrell said. "We were able to slide in and execute the mission pretty much before the North Koreans got out of bed."

"Agreed," Stratemeyer said. "Sorry about the loss to your flight, though. Two downed by anti-aircraft fire and three by MiGs?"

"Only one by anti-aircraft fire, sir. Four by those damn MiGs," Bohn added.

"That's a concern." Stratemeyer frowned. "We didn't anticipate those bastards operating that effectively at night. We can expect more of that as we move on to our next mission."

"Yes, sir," Bohn replied. "We were surprised as hell to see them. They'll be trying to ruin our next run, for sure.

Any chance our fighters can get staged a bit closer to help out?"

"Ray?" Stratemeyer said, looking at Colonel Montrell. Montrell nodded. "The F-86s are no match for the MiG-15s. But Fighter Command tells me they've come up with a new flight procedure that will negate the superiority of the MiG."

"Will they fly at night?" Stratemeyer asked.

"That's a big part of the plan. They're wearing out the runways at Hickam working on it. And keeping all the tourists up at night."

"Strategic bombing of Wonsan is the next mission. Will they be ready?" Stratemeyer needed the F-86s to reduce the losses of the B-29s.

"I believe they will be General," Montrell said. "They're going to be carrier-based and will be as close to the mission area as possible."

Stratemeyer looked at Lt. Col. Bohn. "Are you in on this, Hank?"

"We are, sir. We've got three of our copilots at Hickam now. There's also some carrier brass at Hickam, and they're all working together to assure our B-29s get the protection they need. Those MiGs will get a nasty surprise the next time they fly up to meet us."

General Stratemeyer was curious. "What did you think of those Navy fly boys, Bohn? You ready to switch services?"

Bohn, who had previously accompanied the group to Hickam, laughed. "Hell no, General. First, they hauled me out to this aircraft carrier at night in a damn helicopter. I thought for sure I was a goner. But they got me on board okay. The next day, they waltzed me all over the damn thing, showing me every little part of it. Course, it's as big as Honolulu, so it took most of the damn day."

"They are enormous."

"Yes, sir. They kept me up all of the next night in

the tower, watching as these crazy bastards tried to take off and land on the damn thing. Now mind you, it's pitch black, the seas are rolling like a bowl of soup tossed in a deli, and the wind is blowing like a son of a bitch."

Stratemeyer laughed. "They put on a good show for you."

"They did, sir. I'm just doing my best to hang onto the damn railing without falling on my ass, and this Navy commander is watching all this shit, smiling like a baboon. And these deck hands? They're running all over the place wearing different colored shirts, waving flashlights and acting quite insane."

"Did our naval brethren land their birds okay?"

"They landed every damn one of those birds. I guess about once a week one of them gets splashed, but that night they all made it. One missed the hook and skidded to the end of the ship, which of course is as long as a skyscraper is tall. But the deck crew chased him down with some kind of weird forklift and put a hook on the bird before it could tip into the water. The whole thing looks like bedlam, but those crazy bastards know what they're doing. So no thank you, sir. I'll stick with the Air Force. Our runways usually stay in one place."

"That's great. Keep me in the loop on their progress. Wonsan's only one week away."

"Will do, sir."

***

Bohn's flight of nineteen B-29s initiated what they referred to as the scattered pattern bombing procedure over the night sky of Wonsan. As always, heavy anti-aircraft fire greeted the incoming Superfortresses ten minutes into their attack. Almost every B-29 had been pockmarked with shrapnel from the previous missions. The sheet metal crew in Okinawa worked twenty-four hours a day, patching the bombers.

"Good job, bombardier." Bohn was satisfied with the whole mission. As the flight leader, his aircraft went into a holding pattern until all the B-29s completed their bombing runs.

Before the last B-29 completed his run, twelve MiG-15s arrived and positioned themselves over the B-29 flight group. Unlike the previous missions, however, the MiGs soon found themselves targeted as twenty-four F-86s dropped out of their holding pattern and scattered the MiGs like flies off a rib roast.

"Yee haw!" Bohn yelled over the radio. "The good guys are here." His aircraft had a ringside seat, and the whole crew cheered and shouted as they watched the F-86s go to work. The faster MiGs soon regrouped but every time they attempted to maneuver into position, they found two of the pesky F-86s on their tail. When the bombing was completed, not one B-29 was lost to ack-ack or MiG fire. And although two F-86s were shot down, seven MiG-15s were destroyed and five more were damaged significantly.

Bohn thanked the F-86 flight leader and headed the bomber flight back to Okinawa.

CHAPTER 14

NORTH OF PUSAN

U.S. MARINES 5TH MARINE REGIMENT

Chibenashi Redmond and his new belter sat in the hide. The company had advanced fifty miles in just three days, pushing North Koreans as they went.

"I'm sorry about Mr. Ortiz. I know he was your friend," Private Abe Heiglman said.

"Thanks, but he was just Corporal Ortiz. No mister about it. He was a damn good soldier and a better friend." Despite earlier misgivings, Chibenashi recognized Heiglman as a fine trooper, proficient when it came to feeding belts through the .50 caliber machine gun.

A slightly built Jewish man from New York, Heiglman was somewhat taciturn compared to the jubilant Jim Ortiz. However, when it came to fighting, Heiglman was no wallflower. In several instances after the .50 Cal went silent, Heiglman picked up his M1 and went after the remaining North Koreans as if they had kidnapped his firstborn.

Curious, Chibenashi asked Abe about it. "You seem to have a real hard-on for these bastards, buddy."

Momentarily quiet, Abe finally spoke up. "My father was a POW in a Japanese camp during the war. He was captured in Manchuria and transferred to Korea. After the commies took over in 1945 the bastards used POWs as slave labor until they dropped dead, instead of releasing them as promised."

"Sorry to hear that. Was your dad a Marine?"

"No, Father was an Army accountant who worked in the financial department."

"What the hell was he doing in Manchuria?"

"That's a long story. When we first got involved in the war, we sent tons of aid to China, to support their activities against the Japanese. Over time, millions of dollars of aid came up missing. So the Army sent a special team to try to figure out where the hell everything was going. My father, being an officer and an audit specialist, was lead administrator."

"Did they send any grunts along to deal with the bad guys?" Chibenashi asked.

"Only one small squad. The operation wasn't supposed to get near any of the rough stuff. But as it turned out, they were very much in danger. The communists were fighting the Nationalist Chinese at the same time they were fighting the Japs. And they were stealing the place blind. When the investigating team discovered this, the damn commies jumped 'em and took 'em prisoner."

"So, how'd they end up with the Japs?"

"The Chinese commies wanted to hide their thievery, of course. They didn't want their golden goose to end up in the cook pot. So they destroyed all the accounting reports and secretly informed on them to the nearest Japanese magistrate. He agreed to take the prisoners for a cut in the loot. They sent my dad and the others to the work camps, where they all eventually died."

"How'd anyone find out about all this?" Chibenashi asked.

"The head of the Japanese work camp wanted the American prisoners to set up a dummy operation. The materials being shipped to the Chinese would be cloaked and sent to the Japanese camp instead. Turns out the Jap in charge of the work camp kept meticulous records, including a diary. Eventually, when the camp was overrun by the Chinese Nationalists, they shared the information with our military."

"Wow. The crooks always seem to take over," Chibenashi observed. "What did your dad do before the war?"

"He was a stock broker. He bought and sold shares of commodities, primarily on the New York Stock Exchange."

"Sounds like a good way to make a living."

Abe agreed. "We were very well off—wealthy actually. But I'd give it all up a hundred times over to see dad just one more time."

"Damn, I'm sorry about your dad. Now I understand."

"Thanks, Bird. Say, did you get a letter from your wife?" Chibenashi smiled. "Yep, everyone's doing fine. Morning Star says our son is teething and he started chewing on the table legs. Says we should call him Little Beaver instead of Arnold. And she says he's getting into everything, including my smoking material. She's afraid he'll burn the lodge down."

Family was important to Abe as well. "That must be hard for her, too, trying to raise the kid on her own."

"Yeah. But you know what's great? Nimkii—that's our tribal chief—is taking little Arnold under his wing. He did that during World War Two for the military families. He's teaching Arnold the old ways. My son will make a fine warrior someday."

"Just like his daddy," Abe noted. "What else did she say?"

"I'll skip the mushy stuff...let's see...last of all, they're planning a big celebration for when I get home."

Before Abe could reply, Ike Fenton appeared. "I just want to say you boys are doing fine together. I wrote a letter to Jim's mother, by the way, if you'd like to add anything, Bird. Let me know."

"Thank you, Major, I appreciate that. I also wrote her a letter."

Fenton put his hand on Chibenashi's shoulder. "Good. That's good. We're pulling out tomorrow morning. The main North Korean force is evacuating like rats, but artillery is going to give them a nice little send-off to hurry them on their way. We'll be leaving in trucks and won't be returning to this area, so pack everything but the fire. Be ready to move out at 0600 tomorrow."

***

The company moved north, pushing the North Koreans hard and keeping them on the run for several weeks before NKPA reinforcements arrived. Now the Marines had come under heavy fire again, as wave after wave of North Koreans attacked. They'd been at it for twenty-four hours. Chibenashi and Abe worked the .50 caliber heavy gun almost nonstop.

"I gotta make another ammo run, Bird."

Three times now, Chibenashi had to feed the gun as well as fire it, while the fleet-footed Heiglman ran back for ammo belts. Each time Bird was astonished at the amount of ammunition the small fellow could carry.

"Okay. At the count of five," Bird said, and then counted. Abe dashed out of their small nest as fast as his legs would carry him.

Having seen this drill before, NKPA troops trained their weapons on Abe, who had managed to avoid the intense fire. Within fifteen minutes, Heiglman jumped back into the hide, looking like a Christmas tree festooned with strands of ammunition.

Relieved, Chibenashi let out a long breath and concentrated on firing the weapon. Before long, Captain Fenton appeared and dove into their hide, squeezing the two like packed sardines.

"The Corsairs are coming in ten minutes. We need to pull back just before they do, so we don't get our asses blown off as well." Fenton started to leave and turned back. "You guys are doing a great job. Keep it up."

Chibenashi looked at his watch. "Okay, then. We pull back at exactly 1300 hours."

Abe gave him a sheepish look.

Chibenashi laughed. "One o'clock, Abe."

The two continued to fire the weapon until the appointed time, when Chibenashi grabbed Abe and they bolted from their nest with the heavy gun and unused ammunition belts. They gathered with the rest of the company in a stand of trees about two-hundred yards back.

"What's wrong?" Chibenashi reacted to the long faces and silence from the men who'd arrived ahead of them.

"Fenton got hit," one of them volunteered.

Abe lowered his voice. "Is he...dead?"

The man shook his head. "No, but he's hit pretty bad. I wouldn't bet on his chances."

Chibenashi lowered his head. "Fucking war. Fucking damn war."

***

Gunnery Sergeant Hiram Dent was in a foul mood. "I ain't answering to no niggra."

Major Arthur Girard, Ike Fenton's OIC, got right in Hiram's face. "This outfit is short of officers, Dent. It's not short of gunnery sergeants. So if you are refusing a direct order, I'll have no problem sending your sorry ass back to the States, where you will go up against a court-martial."

Looking around, Girard addressed the whole company. "Headquarters has sent First Lieutenant Devon Hughes as Ike's replacement. Anyone who wants to join Dent in jail, speak up now. Otherwise, act like the Marines you are and support your new officer in charge." Girard turned to Dent. "What's it gonna be Dent? Carry out your duty as a Marine or dishonorable discharge and the brig? Your call."

Clenching his jaw, Dent replied, "I'll do my duty as ordered, sir."

"Good. Glad to hear it." Girard told him. "Your next order is to bring Lieutenant Hughes up to date on the company status."

Back in their tent, Bird and Abe discussed the latest development.

"Next thing you know, we'll be seeing Jews in the officer corps," Heiglman quipped.

"And Indians," Bird added.

"You think Dent will support him?" Abe chuckled.

Chibenashi shook his head. "Hard to say. Dent's a real hard-ass, and he's not too crazy about anyone who isn't lily white from Podunk, USA. I guess time will tell."

"You seem to get along with him," Heiglman said.

"Wasn't always that way. When I first got into the unit, Dent rode me a lot. Called me Geronimo and gave me every shit detail that came along."

"He doesn't ride you much now. What changed?"

"One day we were stuck in a hide together. Dent didn't say much, but I could tell he wasn't thrilled to be in there with me. We were taking fire on and off all day—skirmishers who would only show themselves for a couple seconds before skedaddling back into the bush. I was working the fifty Cal and he was feeding belts. All of a sudden, these two commies jump into our hide. They were short of ammo, as usual, so instead of shooting they tried to bayonet us. Dent got nicked in the arm pretty good, and I ended up fighting them off myself. I killed one with my trenching shovel and knocked the other one out. Since that day, Dent's pretty much left me alone."

Abe now understood. "Impressive, maybe Lieutenant Hughes will have to pop a couple commies to make Dent happy."

"Not sure about that. As much as Dent hates black people, Hughes might have to win the war single-handedly to get Dent off his ass."

CHAPTER 15

"What the hell?" Mario Crucianelli muttered.
Gustav Dietz came over to see what had gotten Mario's attention.

The two were out on patrol and, as usual, they were pushing small groups of North Korean troops farther north, occasionally skirmishing with them.

Dietz to was astonished. "Damn! It's Peg-Leg."

Mario and Dietz locked onto the trail of one boot print accompanied with a round impression.

"These are fresh tracks," Mario whispered.

The two followed the unusual trail while warily keeping an eye out for other NKPA troops. It wasn't long before they came upon a frail North Korean soldier in a ragged uniform, barely shuffling along. No other troops were within sight, and the man was in such poor condition, Mario and Dietz were able to walk right up and disarm him.

The Korean, who had one leg supported on a crude wooden peg as a result of a missing foot, appeared to be a boy of no more than fifteen. He was almost unconscious and hardly took notice as the two searched him and pushed him to the ground.

Mario looked at Dietz. "You know the major's policy on prisoners."

Dietz had a look of concern. "We...we cannot shoot this poor child."

"Well, we sure as hell can't take him back. In his condition, he's gonna die soon anyway, so why not just leave the fucker here?"

Dietz slowly shook his head. "When I was taken prisoner, I saw many men such as this. I was one of them! This, but for the grace of God, would be me. But you Americans...you great people...you picked me up. You treated my wounds and you fed me. Then you took me to a prison camp in America, where I learned a trade and got a chance to become a human being once again."

Mario didn't like where this was going. "What's your point, Gus? We can't take this guy with us. Period."

"But maybe we can take him to the United Nations first aid station."

"How the fuck will we do that? The closest U.N. aid station is probably thirty miles away. The major ain't gonna tolerate us taking a fucking leave of absence to babysit an NKPA commie who's dying. We better get back to the rest of the platoon pretty quick. Leave this guy some water and chuck, and let's get the hell out of here."

"You go. I catch up."

"You'll have both our asses in a sling."

"How's your little boy, Mario?"

"What the fuck does this have to do with him?" Mario asked incredulously. Mario often spoke of his wife and little Andrew. He'd even told Dietz he hoped to introduce them after all the fighting was over and they were back home.

"This boy has a mother and father somewhere. They are waiting for him to come home."

"Yes Gus, and I can assure you that same mother and father are hoping the two of us do not make it home."

"I'm going to carry him back with us. You can shoot me if you like," Dietz picked the boy up and started walking.

Crucianelli was exasperated. "Tobin sent us out here to kill these bastards, not bring 'em back to babysit. He's gonna go ape shit."

"I'll take my chances, Mario. You can go your own way and try to stay out of trouble if you want. I'm taking him back."

***

Major Jack Tobin fumed.

"Where did you say those fuckups went, Private?"

"Maybe I misunderstood them, sir." Private Darren Lamoure stared at the ground.

Tobin got right up in Lamoure's face. "Where did they tell you they were going before you misunderstood them?"

"The U.N. station, sir." Lamoure trembled.

"Where?"

"They said they were taking their wounded prisoner to the U.N. station...sir."

"And you let 'em go," Tobin looked around at the rest of the platoon, he added.

One of the other men spoke up. "Sir, we weren't exactly in a position to stop them. We had our own wounded to take care of."

Tobin just shook his head. "I'm sending five of you dumb bastards after them. When they're back, I'm gonna arrest them for desertion. If the five dumb fucks I send out come back without those two, I'll arrest those five for dereliction of duty. Any questions?"

Ten miles away Mario Crucianelli, Gustav Dietz, and their prisoner slowly made their way to what they believed to be a U.N. headquarters. After watching Dietz almost collapse, a frustrated Mario agreed to take turns carrying the injured prisoner.

"Tobin will have us court-martialed."

"We'll be shot for desertion."

"Better to die an honorable man, than to let a wounded child die, Mario."

Carrying the wounded youth, Mario grunted. "That'll look great on our headstones."

Two hours later, the men neared the area where they thought the U.N. headquarters was stationed.

"Halt!" A patrol of blue-helmeted men in crisp, clean uniforms surrounded them.

Mario and Dietz stopped and lowered their captive to the ground. Recognizing the men as German, Dietz conversed with them in his native tongue.

"What the fuck, Gus. Did you run into some relatives out here?"

"These are United Nation troops from West Germany. They're going to take us to their headquarters. There's a hospital that can treat this boy."

"Find out if they've got a couple of nice caskets to ship our bodies home after Tobin has us shot," Mario quipped.

"They're taking us into custody. We won't have to worry about getting shot for a while," Dietz informed him.

"Custody?" Crucianelli was incredulous.

A man who appeared to be in charge addressed the two. "Yes, we are taking you into custody. Mistreatment of prisoner of war, you're coming with us. Now."

***

With a lull in the fighting, Major Tobin left a company captain in charge and went to the U.N. facility to tend to the matter himself. He then visited the two, who were being held in a tent under twenty-four-hour guard.

"I told you boneheads 'no prisoners.' Did you not understand my order? Do you see what's happened as a result of your ill-advised rescue mission?"

While Crucianelli stood mute, Dietz offered a rebuttal. "We cannot treat the prisoners like animals—"

"They are the enemy, Dietz." Tobin cut in. "Our job is to dispatch them, not to set up some half-assed rescue mission for juvenile offenders. The Russians slaughtered German and Italian prisoners by the thousands. They knew how to conduct a war."

"The Russians are pigs, Major."

"Didn't you learn anything on that farm in Wisconsin, Dietz? Pigs are pretty smart."

Crucianelli spoke up. "Do you know what's going to happen to us, Major?"

"No. Dietz here has fixed your clock good. While you guys have been eating bratwurst, drinking beer, and fraternizing with your new Kraut friends, they've been building a case against you. Or us, I should say. They intend to file formal charges of prisoner abuse with the United Nations general counsel. Against our entire unit."

This caught Dietz off guard.

"I do not understand. I explained that we found the man in the condition he was in and brought him in for treatment."

Tobin smirked. "It seems your 'patient' told the Germans otherwise. He claims you beat him within an inch of his life and whacked his foot off with your trenching shovel."

While Dietz was flummoxed, Crucianelli was enraged.

"That little bastard! We carried that fucker halfway across Korea to a cushy U.N. hospital and he throws us to the wolves?"

Tobin was almost laughing. "No good deed, boys. No good deed."

"I want to talk to him," Dietz said.

"Won't happen." Tobin shook his head. "The Krauts have set him up with a pretty little U.N. lawyer, and she's got you guys in the crosshairs."

"What's next?" Mario asked.

"I don't have an answer for that," Tobin replied. "It was my intention to haul your asses back to our outfit, where you'd be thrown into the brig and court-martialed. But the U.N. has complete authority over the case now, and who knows what these fucking European wackos will do with you. Either way, you're in a pile of dung thirty feet high."

CHAPTER 16

Colonel Montrell now sat with Henry Bohn. "Wonsan was well-executed, Hank".

"Thanks, Ray. The air crews deserve a big chunk of the credit. It was a collaborative effort that made the mission a success. And I don't have to tell you what a great job those F-86s did."

"That they did," Montrell agreed. "I already called Suwon and thanked them."

That surprised Bohn. "I thought Suwon was overrun. My news must be old."

"It was overrun, but we've already taken the base back, and the F-86s are flying around the clock again."

"Those North Korean MiG pilots are getting pretty scarce," Bohn noted.

Montrell nodded. "That's good news and bad news. Word has it that the Soviets and Red Chinese are sending pilots down to make up for the losses."

"I'm okay with that. I'd like nothing better than to splash a bunch of Russkie and Chink pilots."

Montrell wasn't so sure about that. "I'd like that as well, but the Chinese—and particularly the Russian—pilots are much more skilled than the North Koreans. Might be a tougher nut to crack next time around. Of course, those

116

F-86 Sabre pilots are all nuts, anyway. I think they'd be happy if they were facing ten-to-one odds. How are the repairs coming, Hank?"

Most of the wing's B-29s had been "salt and peppered" by anti-aircraft fire. Maintenance crews worked day and night, patching up the holes, but it was a never-ending task. "All but five are ready to go. Not sure if any of those five are salvageable though. Might have to get some new ones over here."

Montrell shook his head. "Command says we aren't going to see anything new until the next model is released." "Better send us some B-24s then. Otherwise we'll be dropping bombs one at a time from those Sabre jets."

"We'll be all right, Hank. Command tells me we've got seven rebuilt B-29s coming in from Guam, and they're as good as new."

"Excellent. Happy to hear that, we'll get them just in time for the mission to Nampojin. We'll break them in right."

"Good deal. And safe wings there, Hank. Safe wings."

CHAPTER 17

"Where the fuck are they coming from?" Abe wanted to know.

Never having heard Abe swear before, Chibenashi actually stopped firing the .50 Cal for a second and looked over at him. NKPA troops had mounted charge after charge for the better part of three hours. Abe's hands were bleeding from stuffing belts into the weapon. Chibenashi had to keep slapping his trigger hand, as it kept going numb.

"We may have to bug out." Chibenashi warned. "We'll be short of ammo again soon, and even your fast, little ass won't be able to get in and out of here quick enough."

"As bad as these fuckers shoot, I'm not worried about it."

The NKPA soldiers were armed with the standard Russian World War II carryover weapon, a bolt action 7.2 mm carbine. The guns were not exceptionally accurate or dependable.

Chibenashi had other concerns. "I'm not too worried about their shooting ability, but it looks like some of them are carrying grenades. They don't have to be too damn accurate with those."

No sooner had Chibenashi spoken than ten NKPA troops rushed the machine gun nest, grenades in hand. Abe feverishly fed the ammo belts, while Bird mowed seven of them down before they could get within range to toss the grenades. Three pushed through the intense fire from the .50 cal. While one was cut down just as he was ready to throw his grenade, the other two managed to toss theirs into the nest.

One of the grenades bounced out but detonated close enough to wound both men. As Abe and Chibenashi writhed in pain, the other grenade rolled into the middle of their nest. Chibenashi pushed Abe aside and jumped on top of the grenade just as it detonated.

CHAPTER 18

"So that little fucker changed his tune," Major Tobin said.

Kim Jun-Son, the young NKPA soldier who had been taken to the U.N. hospital by Mario and Gus, had finally told the truth at the trial where the two Americans were repeatedly grilled by zealous European prosecuting attorneys. Gustav Dietz and Mario Crucianelli were acquitted of abusing a prisoner of war in a United Nations court of law.

Mario finally found some sympathy for the young Korean caught up in the war. "Yeah. He's not any kind of dyed-in-the-wool commie or anything. Just another lost soul in this shitty fucking war. He was ingrained with hate for us and led to believe we were mother-killing monsters."

"I sure as hell wouldn't be so forgiving," Tobin scoffed.

"But since you and Dietz here have been living the high life, I guess you've gone soft on me. That is, you've gone soft Mario. Dietz here has always been a hand-wringer."

Mario was losing patience with his sarcastic OIC. "Thanks, Major. Your unending support and keen wit are always appreciated."

"Anytime. Now, I have some more news you may want to hear."

"Let's have it, Major." Mario sucked in a lungful of air in preparation for the gut-punch. He and Dietz were expecting a court-martial with a possible prison sentence to go along with it.

Looking at both Dietz and Crucianelli, Major Tobin delivered his news. "You are being discharged—both of you. You'll be sent back to the States after you've been out-processed. I expect that to take three days, no more."

Both men spoke up at the same time. "What kind of discharge?"

Tobin's demeanor changed. "I've leaned on you two quite a bit, I know. The truth is you were both damn good soldiers, and I hated the idea of losing you. When you took off with that kid, I felt like you let me down. After the trial and thinking on it more, I agree with the findings of United States Army Command, Korea."

"And what are those findings, sir?" Dietz wasn't sure he really wanted to know the answer to his question.

"That your actions reflect the best traditions of the United States Army. You risked your lives for an individual who was your enemy—a wounded enemy, but an enemy just the same. In the exact words of the command's report: 'This is who American soldiers are.' Your discharge will be honorable. And you'll receive commendation medals for your actions to save your prisoner." Tobin paused and said softly, "Good job, men, and safe travels back home."

Dietz and Mario let out a sigh of relief. "And good luck to you as well, sir," they echoed.

PART 3

*Like blowing sand in the desert, our experiences
gather in ever growing hills over our lifetime.*

A Period of Recovery before the Winds of War Return

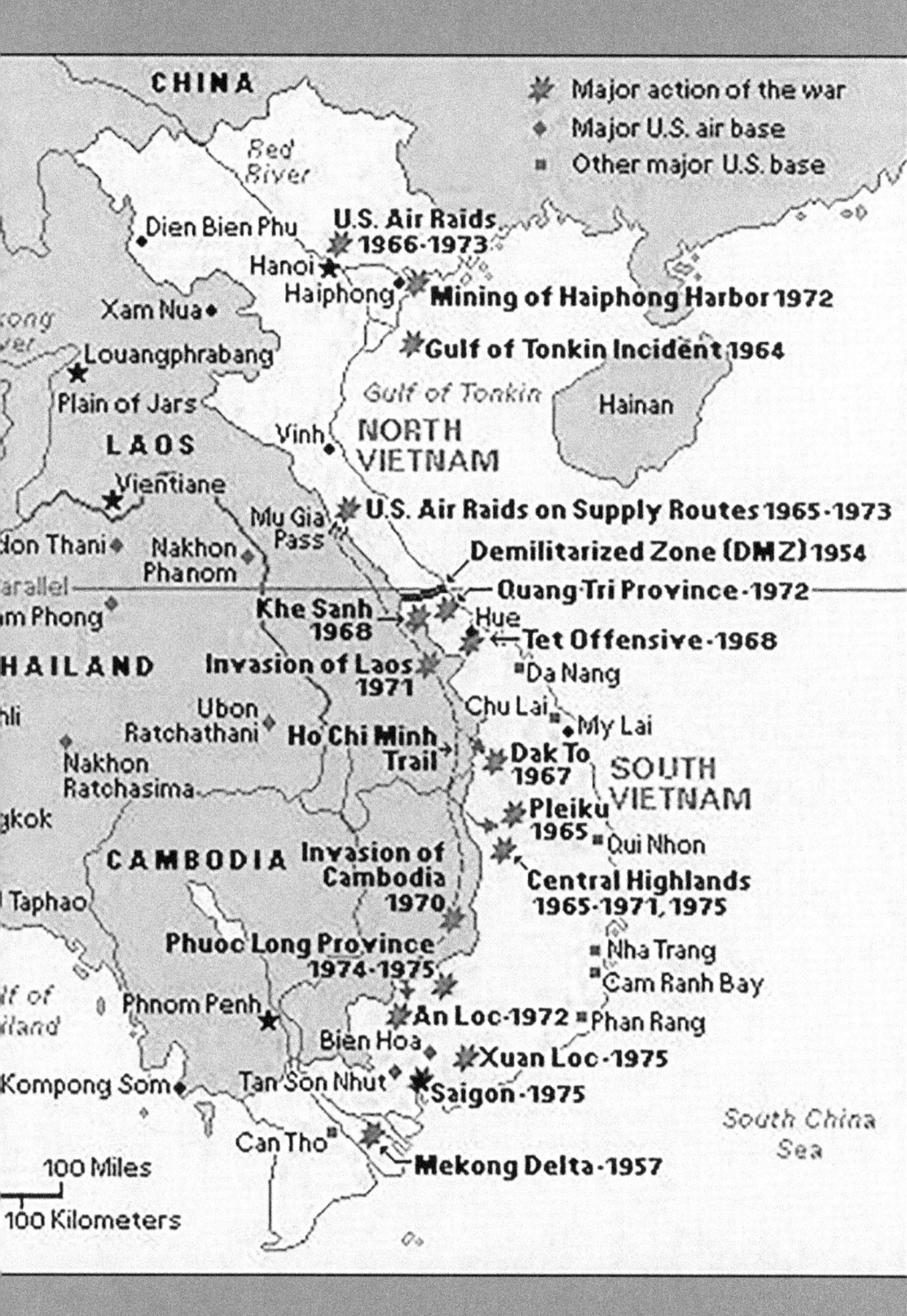

CHAPTER 19

WHITE EARTH INDIAN RESERVATION, MINNESOTA

Ishkode Redmond watched his nephew Arnold playing in the dirt outside their little shack. It had been five years since Arnold's father, Chibenashi, was killed in action while serving in Korea. Arnold's mother, Morning Star, worked six days a week, ten hours a day at the Ojibwa tribal administration building, performing janitorial services.

Ishkode sat Arnold down. "You are seven-years old now, little Mukwa. It's time you started learning the ways."

Having lost his leg while fighting in the Pacific during World War II, Ishkode now received a small pension from the U.S. government. Between Morning Star's wages and Ishkode's pension, the three had just enough money to purchase food, clothing, and Ishkode's quart of whiskey every other day.

"I want to play, Zhishay." Arnold protested, using the Ojibwa term for uncle. "And I'm not a bear."

"Well, you eat like one." Ishkode laughed. "You better get studying that book your mother gave you or she'll punish both of us."

"I don't like the books, no one looks like us," Arnold complained. The federal government doled out learning materials to tribal residents along with their monthly allotment coupons for their basic needs. The learning books for children depicted blond, blue-eyed youth with never-ending smiles on their faces.

"Do you want me to paint them brown?" Ishkode teased.

"They don't play our games," Arnold also pointed out.

"You can learn from them anyway. Don't be like Lightfeather's mule." Ishkode said, referring to the neighbor's mule, which had never done anything willingly as far as anyone could tell.

"He doesn't like the books either?"

Laughing, Ishkode tousled Arnold's hair. "Go get me my medicine now, young cub."

"Mother told me not to."

Ishkode frowned. "Your mother doesn't know how badly I need it. If you won't get it, give me my sticks and I will get it myself."

Arnold ran inside and opened Ishkode's cupboard, which contained his tobacco, leg ointment, several old books, his military medals, some letters from Arnold's father Chibenashi, and a bottle of cheap whiskey, half full. Arnold sifted through his father's letters, gently feeling the paper and bringing them up to his nose to smell.

"Are you lost, little cub?" Ishkode yelled.

Arnold returned with the bottle.

"Thank you, Arnold. Now go look at your books."

"Yes, Uncle." Arnold replied quietly, watching Ishkode take a long pull on the bottle.

***

"The white man has taken Arnold away from us Ishkode," Morning Star announced after returning from a tribal council hearing.

The Indian agent from the state had served papers informing Morning Star that reports from the local agent indicated Arnold Redmond was not being properly cared for. Pending the decision of the council, he would be removed from the reservation and relocated to a boarding house where Native American children at risk were housed. The children would be taught in a local school which provided no consideration regarding their own culture.

Ishkode sat mute for a time. "It's my fault. It was my job to tend to him while you were at work. I am nothing but a damn reservation drunk."

Morning Star did not feel compelled to argue with him. "What will we do?" Ishkode asked.

Morning Star's anger prompted sarcasm. "I will go to the tribal council to appeal. You will get drunk and pass out...like you always do, every day."

"Not every day," Ishkode protested.

Morning Star did not flinch. "Yes. Every day."

The news depressed Ishkode. He loved Arnold as much as if he were his own son. And he knew the spirit of his brother Chibenashi would be ashamed and angry with him. If only he hadn't lost his leg. The Marine Corps was the only place he'd ever felt at home, and when he could no longer serve it broke his spirit.

"I will go with you, Morning Star."

Morning Star shook her head. "That will not make the white man any happier."

"What can I do?" Ishkode asked in desperation.

"You can get sober and become the man you were before the poison you drink captured your spirit."

***

The hearing to determine the fate of young Arnold Redmond took place at the same tribal administration building where Morning Star Redmond was employed. Her coworkers sneered at the intrusive white men in their drab suits and worn briefcases. The agency representatives were here in response to Morning Star's appeal.

"What information have you brought for us, Mrs. Redmond?"

"I have a new caregiver for Arnold. She will be with him every moment while I am at work."

Harold Becker, the agent in charge, looked down at his paperwork. "Is this person an adult?"

"Yes, her name is Miiwan. She is my mother."

"Does this person use alcohol?" Becker's tone was icy.

Morning Star stiffened "My mother does not drink alcohol."

"Will Ishkode Redmond be on the premises?"

"Ishkode has gone away."

"Will he still be spending time in your home, Mrs. Redmond?"

"Ishkode has gone to live with relatives of the Fond du Lac band. We will not see him again."

Becker nodded. "We will take this new information into consideration and make a determination."

"When can Arnold come home?" Morning Star asked.

"If the board determines your home and arrangements are now appropriate, Arnold will be back in your home within the month."

CHAPTER 20

1955

JANESVILLE, WISCONSIN

Mario Crucianelli finished his shift at the General Motors plant in Janesville, Wisconsin. From ten at night until seven in the morning, Mario assembled bumpers for Chevrolet automobiles and pick-up trucks. He was happy with his job, which paid a decent wage, along with some benefits. It supported him, his wife, and their child. With another baby on the way, Mario hoped to acquire some overtime hours so the family could put a down payment on a little Cape Cod home in the new subdivision on the edge of town. When he got home to their little apartment, his wife Delia announced that the landlord had stopped by.

"What does he want now? Another damned rent increase?"

"No, he came to tell you that your friend Gus called, and to call him back when you get a chance."

The one-bedroom apartment in the two-flat consisted of a kitchen with a table, a living room, a bedroom, and a small bathroom. It had electricity as well as the recently supplied natural gas service. Telephone lines were not yet available.

Mario nodded. "I'll go to Kresge's before I get some shut-eye. Do we need anything while I'm there?"

The department store, about three miles away, had two public phones, kept busy by the many residents in the area without phone service of their own.

"Just some more cough medicine for Andrew. Don't get lost."

Mario's son Andrew had whooping cough. His loud "whoops" could be heard through the paper-thin walls of their little apartment.

"Is Mrs. Wirtz complaining again?"

"No, but we're getting low and I don't want to run out in the middle of the night."

Mario purchased the medicine and waited for two people to finish their calls before he could telephone his old friend Gustav Dietz. Dietz had moved back to Wisconsin after he was discharged from military service. He went back to work on the farm where he'd worked before he enlisted. "What's up, Gus? Did they throw you back in prison yet?"

"They would not do that to a gentleman like me. Are you still welding bumpers on the wrong side of those Chevrolets?"

"No, I got a promotion. I bolt 'em on with an air gun, now. Shoots better than those junk carbines we had in Korea. What's up, buddy?"

"The milking parlor is shut down for repairs. I thought it would be a good time to teach you how to fish properly."

"I'll out-fish you any time. Where are you going?"

"I got a nice little spot on the Wisconsin River where I catch catfish and a few walleye, also. We can pitch my tent and stay the whole weekend. You can bring Andrew, too. I'll bring the beer 'cause all you drink is that crappy Schlitz."

"Man, I'd love to come. Sounds like a great time. But Andrew's got the damn whooping cough, and I'm working weekends trying to save money so Delia and I can get a house and maybe a business to go along with it."

"Poor Andrew. Whooping cough is bad. You must burn paper in a glass on his chest to chase it out," Dietz advised, remembering the old-world cure from his childhood.

"I don't think that'll fly. Delia would murder me if I put a torch to that kid. You ever heard of antibiotics, buddy?"

Dietz scoffed. "Ach! Those doctors will kill you with their potions. I will stick to the old ways, my friend. Well, sorry you can't go fishing. You could have added some more lies to your collection."

Mario laughed. "Next time, buddy. You'll have to cook up some new stories for the both of us this time around."

***

As Mario headed home from work at the GM plant, he decided to treat himself to a daily newspaper so he could read about his beloved Chicago Cubs. He never tired of hearing about them and watched them play baseball every chance he got.

Things had been going well for Mario and his young family. He'd been picking up enough overtime at the GM plant to put away money each month for a down payment on the new home they hoped to purchase.

Looking toward a brighter future, Mario and Delia started a little cottage industry, selling homemade Italian sausage, pickled wild mushrooms, and bakery goods to locals in the neighborhood as well as three nearby delicatessens. They hoped to open a store of their own at some point.

"Mario, how very nice to see you."

Looking up from his newspaper, Mario felt a chill down his back. Fortunato Calabrese was a local hood. Originally from Chicago, he'd moved to the Janesville area to shake down workers at the prosperous GM plant. His activities included loan sharking, gambling, and the protection racket.

"Oh...good morning, Fortunato. Nice to see you also," Mario lied.

"I was so very happy to learn about the fine wares you and your lovely wife are selling. I have purchased several bottles of my favorite, the pickled mushrooms, at Guidotti's market."

"Glad you like them," Mario mumbled.

Fortunato soon got to the point. "Mario, allow me to explain my meeting up with you today. As a businessman, you understand how important it is to protect your assets. I can provide you with insurance for your business...to protect you in the event of any type of pressure from unscrupulous competitors, for example."

Mario hoped to divert the issue. "Delia and I have been lucky. Our very small business has not experienced any such pressure. But thank you for your kind offer."

"Why you are too modest, Mario. Of course, I've looked into this matter. For instance, in addition to Guidotti's you also enjoy a thriving trade with Molinaro's Deli and Pachetto's Fine Foods. If you include all the business you conduct with your neighbors, you should have an insurance policy worth a fee of...oh...I'd say around a hundred dollars a month." Fortunato leaned in. "I will start collecting on the first day of next month. That gives you two weeks to make the funds ready."

Mario hoped there was a way out. "That's very gracious of you, Fortunato. But what if I don't wish to purchase such a policy at this time?"

Fortunato's eyes turned cold. "Businessmen without this insurance have had many misfortunes, Mario. Fires, thefts, and even assaults have befallen them. I would not wish to see that happen to you and your family...capisce?"

Mario bowed his head in surrender. "I understand."

***

"Catfish are holding out on us, Mario."

Taking a rare weekend off, Mario sat next to Gus on the banks of the Wisconsin River in Central Wisconsin.

Gustav felt something was amiss. Mario wasn't his usual chipper self. He wasn't even paying attention to his line, which was now tighter than a drawn bowstring.

"Looks like you got one interested," Dietz noted.

Mario half-heartedly set the hook, but the fish got away. Looking at him seriously, Dietz finally asked, "Mario, what's bothering you my friend?"

Mario took in a long breath and told Dietz all about Fortunato Calabrese and his protection scam.

Dietz shook his head in disbelief. "Does Delia know?"

"No! With her so damn pregnant, I'm afraid she'd lose the baby if she found out."

"Hasn't she noticed the missing money?"

"She has. I told her it was a loan to my worthless cousin Paulie. He's always losing money gambling."

"How long can you keep that up?"

"Till I come up with some way to kill this son of a bitch."

"I will help you. We've killed sons of bitches before."

"Thanks, Gus, but I can't drag you into this. And these guys are like cockroaches. You kill one and ten more crawl out of the woodwork to come after you."

"What about Armando...your cousin?"

During their tour in Korea, Gus and Mario had shared their family histories with each other, including some of their more notorious family members. For his part, Gus revealed that his uncle Franz was a member of the infamous SS, the elite paramilitary corps of the Nazis. Mario had told Gus about his cousin, Armando Mezzolini, a mid-level mobster from Chicago, who worked the rackets along Cicero Avenue. Armando was also an enforcer for the Chicago Outfit's Paul Ricca.

Dietz had touched a nerve with Mario. "I've thought about calling him. Many times, in fact, but you remember what I told you about those guys. Once they get their hooks into you, you're locked into the program from there on out. I'm hoping to resolve this thing on my own."

Dietz was sympathetic to his friend's predicament. "I understand. Whatever happens, I'm here for you and your family. You know that Mario."

"Thanks, that means a lot to me Gus."

CHAPTER 21

"How's the tuna salad, Ray?" Henry Bohn raised his eyebrows.

"Tastes just like tuna salad," Montrell quipped.

"Okay, how about another topic. How're your students doing?"

After the Korean War ended, Boeing lured both Montrell and Bohn out of the Air Force and into lucrative jobs as flight instructors, teaching pilots everything they needed to know about the Boeing 377 Stratocruiser, a derivative of the B-29 bomber.

"I think half of them should stick to spraying crops," Montrell groused. "They don't appear to have any grasp of mathematics or physics. And they don't really give a shit."

Bohn laughed. "This morning one of mine told me if he ever decided to fly to Mars he'd learn trigonometry. Until then, he'd go by the sun, stars, and hills—just like his daddy did."

Montrell shook his head. "You know, half of these guys did some damn good flying over Korea. It's a shame they're going to get bounced out because they can't hit a few books at night."

"Yeah, good thing the military wasn't looking too close, else most of 'em would have ended up as cooks. Well, job security for us, I guess. At the rate we're bouncing 'em out, it'll take ten years to come up with thirty decent aircrews.

You think we should discuss this with management?"

"I do. Most of these guys are working hard—trying to support a family—and they just don't have the hours to put in for study. I've been thinking maybe a pre-flight school learning process would help. Teach them the fundamentals leading into the higher math and science skills required."

"That's a fine idea, but if they don't have time to tackle the studying now, how will they have time under that program?"

"I've thought about that. It would be strictly a learn-at-home program. No time limit assigned. When the individual completed the program in his own time, he'd be tested to determine if he had the knowledge needed to enter flight training. I'd actually like you to help me develop the plan, Hank. If management approves of the idea it and it's implemented, it should boost the success rate of our pilot training significantly."

"Sounds like a good idea. Of course, I'll help."

***

Ray and Hank met with Boeing management to discuss their new training proposal some months later.

"The board has gone over your proposal," said Tom Fitch, Vice President of Technology and Training. "Thanks for bringing this to our attention, boys. At this time Boeing doesn't feel it fits our needs. However, we'll keep the report on file in case conditions change."

Ray nodded. "Okay. Well, thanks, Tom. Appreciate the feedback. May I ask what the rationale for rejection was?" Fitch grimaced. "Management feels the training program you offer would cut into their revenue stream."

That response didn't sit well with Bohn. "So it's all about money."

Fitch held up his hands. "Hank, Boeing invests a lot of time and effort into these training programs. And yes, they expect a specific return for that effort. Our statistical model anticipates the percentage of pilots who will drop out and be replaced by new pilots to fill those slots."

Fitch's response angered Montrell. He struggled to keep his voice even. "So you're banking on a number of men to fail. And of course, the fees they pay in advance are nonrefundable. So Boeing pockets the cash from both the winners and the losers."

"It's just business, Ray. Don't make us out to be the bad guys."

Bohn jumped back in. "Bullshit, Fitch. Most of these guys spent three years getting their asses shot at while you fat cats at Boeing sat back here puffing cigars and drinking brandy. Now when they need a break, Boeing is saying, 'Fuck you.'"

Fitch looked over at Montrell pleadingly, "Ray, help me out here. You understand that Boeing has to make a profit."

"A goddamned obscene profit," Montrell noted.

At that Tom Benninger, Boeing Vice President of Finance stood up. "I recommend we postpone this discussion until further notice. This meeting is adjourned. We're done here, gentlemen."

***

Still fuming over the callous manner in which Boeing treated their pilot trainees, Montrell and Bohn agreed to meet with members of senior management of Lockheed Corporation in Dayton, Ohio. Lockheed had reached out to them multiple times over the years, hoping to lure the two away from Boeing.

Steve Tarbill, Vice President of Engineering, kicked off the meeting with an in-depth discussion on the project at hand.

"Gentlemen, as you were advised earlier, everything you see and hear today is, of course, confidential. It's also classified. I need to remind you that you've both signed documents to that effect. Can you put up the charts, Brenda?"

After Tarbill's assistant set up the overhead projector, Tarbill began his presentation. "Ever since the end of World War Two, we've been keeping an eye on the Russians, using aerial reconnaissance. The Luftwaffe had a considerable number of photographs of the existing Soviet military complexes, and we were able to secure many of them before the end of the war. Since that time, we've been relying on our bombers to do the job, but more and more of them are getting shot down. Boeing's B-47 has been the primary workhorse, but there aren't many left."

The next slide showed a new strange-looking aircraft.

"For the past few years Lockheed engineers and designers have been working with the Air Force in developing an aircraft that could gather photographic data in today's environment. The specifications we were given required an aircraft that could fly over the current Soviet anti-aircraft reach—around seventy thousand feet—with a range of seventeen-hundred miles."

The next slide showed a close-up view of a mock-up of the aircraft.

"The aircraft, designated the CL-282, or U-2 as it is better known, has been selected as the high-altitude reconnaissance aircraft of the future. The chosen pilot instructors will work closely with the engineers, designers, and test pilots to fine tune the machine. After the pilot instructors are familiar with the bird, they'll train Central Intelligence Agency operatives for the job. With your experience, gentlemen, I suspect that some of the men in that group have already been trained by you on other aircraft."

After a quick lunch, the orientation continued for an hour. Then Tarbill gathered his slides and paperwork and left the conference room.

"What do you think, Ray?" Paul Schultz was the Vice President of Human Resources.

"I'm satisfied with your offer for the most part," Montrell said. "The money and benefits are fine. And I'm glad to see that your pilot training program is substantial enough to provide pilots with the skills required for math and the sciences. I do have a couple additional requirements, however."

"Name them," Schultz said.

"Well, first, I'm only interested if Henry agrees to come along with me. We've been a team since World War Two, and I think we function best when we're together."

Schultz turned in his seat. "Henry, what about it? We'd be thrilled to bring both of you on board. What do you say?" Bohn looked up from the contract. "I like the program, I'm in."

"What's number two, Ray?" Schultz asked.

"Don't get me wrong...I like this U-2 program and I like training pilots. But I also have the itch to fly again. I'd like a contract that allows me to become a pilot in the program after three years of instructing."

"We'll have to do some investigative work on that, Ray. I'll need input from the powers that be before I can agree to such a request. As you very well know, top pilot trainers are hard to come by. That's why we've recruited you so insistently over the years. And that's why we're offering such a high paying salary and bonus schedule." Schultz looked over at Bohn. "What about you, Hank? Does that go for you as well?"

"No. I'm happy just to continue training pilots. But Ray's my partner and best friend. If this is a deal breaker for him, it's a deal breaker for me, too. We both come on board or neither of us does."

"I understand," Schultz said. "I'll address this with the board and get back to you both as soon as possible. And again, gentlemen, I must remind you that whatever you or we decide, this information is top secret. Any breach will be treated as a threat to national security."

CHAPTER 22

"**A**rnold, eat your oatmeal."

It had been five weeks since Ishkode left the Redmond household. Morning Star's mother Miiwan took care of young Arnold on the days Morning Star worked. Enjoying a day off, Morning Star had prepared Arnold's favorite breakfast—hot oatmeal with raisins and sugar.

Arnold stirred the oatmeal and frowned. "There's not enough sugar."

"Yes, there is. Too much sugar will rot your teeth young brave. And when are you going to stop all this moping around? Grandmother and I take good care of you. You should be a happy boy."

"I miss Uncle."

"I miss him, too," Morning Star acknowledged. "Ishkode loves us very much and we love him. But because of the sadness in his spirit, he cannot give you proper care and guidance."

"Why is he so sad, Mother?"

Morning Star sat down and held Arnold's hand. "When Uncle lost his leg in the war, he was no longer able to be a Marine. He will always be a warrior, with one leg or two, but the Marines did not agree. They sent him home with medals and letters from important men and enough money every month to feed himself and stay drunk. He wasn't always this bad. He crafted wooden totems and sold them at the Indian store the tourists visit. But when his little brother—your father—was killed, Uncle Ishkode lost another part of himself, even more important than his leg. He lost his spirit."

Arnold thought he understood. "Will Uncle's spirit ever come back?"

"I don't know, Arnold. If Ishkode remembers that he is a warrior and fights the demons that are tormenting him... he may get his spirit back."

***

FOND DU LAC INDIAN RESERVATION, MINNESOTA

"I told you he would be trouble, Nathaniel. You should listen to me." Norma Killdeer, the woman who lived with Nathaniel, nagged him constantly about Ishkode.

"Quiet hen, you give me more trouble than he does.

Maybe you should be the one to leave."

"If I leave, I will take all of my tools with me. You two used-up old roosters will starve to death. It would serve you right."

"I am not that old. And if I throw you out, you will have to find another generous man. He will have to be blind, so he does not have to look at your mean face. And deaf, so he will not have to listen to your squawking all day long."

Norma Killdeer's observations regarding Ishkode were not far off the mark, though. Ishkode Redmond was in the process of killing himself. He'd been drinking and passing out nonstop since arriving at his cousin Nathaniel's home on the Fond du Lac reservation.

Though only in his mid-thirties, Ishkode's haggard appearance suggested a man much older than he actually was. Gaunt, pale, and unsteady on his one leg, Ishkode was aging at an alarming rate. He rarely ate, drank little but whiskey, and appeared outside of the lodge only after the sun went down. In truth, Nathaniel White Bear was already weary of Ishkode's presence.

"Ishkode!" Nathanial shook his cousin. "Ishkode, wake up."

"Run! Run, Mata!" Ishkode stirred and mumbled at the demons tormenting him.

"Mata is okay now, Ishkode. Wake up and let's have some coffee," Nathaniel gently shook Ishkode.

"I need a drink," Ishkode mumbled, half-awake.

Nathaniel shook his head. "No, you do not need a drink. You need some coffee and food, Ishkode. Don't you want to see your family again?"

Ishkode grunted. "The white man says I am not fit."

"And you are proving them right, my friend."

Ishkode sat mute for a long time before speaking. "What can I do Nathaniel?"

***

Ishkode Redmond was nervous. He'd been asked to report to the tribal council room in Fond du Lac Indian Reservation's administration building. Believing he was in trouble, he forced himself to stay sober and cleaned himself up for the meeting. Nathaniel accompanied him.

Arriving at the office, they found one of the tribal leaders waiting there with a white man. Ishkode figured it was an Indian agent, here to meddle.

Don Blue Hawk, the tribal leader, made the introductions, "Ishkode, this is Mr. Harris from the state Indian Health Board. He has some information for you."

"Nice to meet you, Ishkode," Harris extended his hand. "I understand you performed very honorably in the war."

"I did no more than many others but thank you."

Harris continued. "It appears, based on your record, that you have a benefactor."

Ishkode shook his head in confusion. "I'm afraid I don't understand."

"Someone wishes to do something on your behalf," Blue Hawk explained.

"What do they want to do?"

"A person who wishes to remain anonymous has funded an indefinite stay for you at the alcohol abuse center near the Twin Cities," Harris explained. "Every expense will be paid, including your transportation to and from the facility." Ishkode narrowed his eyes. "Why would they do this?"

Harris shook his head. "I don't know, sir, but whoever it is thinks very highly of you. This is an expensive treatment facility, normally attended by only the wealthiest of people.

Ishkode had some doubts. "What if I don't wish to go?"

Before anyone else could respond, Nathaniel White Bear spoke up.

"Then you will be sent back to White Earth in the same miserable condition in which you arrived, because you will no longer be welcome here."

CHAPTER 23

D elia looked up from the bank statement in her hand. "Mario! What is going on?"

For the past three months, Mario had taken one hundred dollars from their precious savings each month, supposedly to send to his cousin Paulie. Delia had held her tongue long enough. A tough farm girl of German ancestry, Delia was raised on a local farm with two sisters and three brothers. She was accustomed to fighting for her place at the table and gave quarter to no one. It's one of the things Mario most admired when they were courting. Now it seemed to be working against him.

"I have to help my cousin, Delia. He's family! If he doesn't pay his debts, the thugs will break his legs."

Gustav had often teased Mario about his wife. "That tough little Kraut is going to beat all the bones out of your skinny Italian body, my friend. Maybe you should turn her over to me."

Mario would fire back. "She would turn you into a pile of that liver sausage you love so much. You'd better stick to those milk cows."

Today Delia was angrier than Mario had ever seen her. "Paulie is a lousy gambler and he doesn't have the brains to stop. I will no longer allow our future to be placed in jeopardy by a man who cannot control his impulses. No more! Do you understand, Mario?"

Not knowing what else to say, Mario slowly nodded.

"I'll tell him tomorrow."

"I know it's a hard thing for you to do, but it's for the best." She changed the subject. "Have you talked to the police about that stranger?"

Even though Mario had been making payments on a regular basis, Fortunato made weekly rounds at the three stores where the Crucianellis sold their wares. He also made visits to their neighborhood. Fortunato Calabrese had been in the rackets for a long time. He never trusted anything to chance and kept a close watch on all of his "business" interests. When he got his hooks into someone, he made sure his presence was felt.

"They say they need a picture of him," Mario lied.

"Well, we can't afford a camera, thanks to Paulie. I'll borrow Mother's next time we're out at the farm."

***

In desperation, Mario Crucianelli finally mustered his nerve and arranged a visit with his notorious cousin, Armando Mezzolini, in Chicago.

"So, my fine cousin, what brings you to Chicago? Did you finally decide to get some real Italian bread?"

They sat on the back porch of Armando's three-story apartment building in the middle of town just off of Cicero Avenue, sipping espresso coffee spiked with Anisette, Grappa's weaker little sister. Every five minutes, their conversation was drowned out by the roar of a nearby passing El train.

"I'm being shaken down by a cheap hood," Mario said, failing to meet Armando's eyes.

Armando contemplated his espresso. "How long has this cheap hood been disrespecting you, Mario?"

Even fortified with liquor, the conversation was difficult for Mario. "It started about five months ago. At first, I thought it was a bad dream, it was such a shock."

Armando raised his eyebrows. "Five months? You

allow this insult to continue for five months before paying your respects to me?”

“I was embarrassed. I should be able to defend my own family and honor. I hoped not to bother you with such a petty complaint.”

Armando pursed his lips. “You figured you fought bravely in Korea, so why not swat this cockroach yourself, eh?”

“Yeah, I guess that’s what I kept thinking, Armando. I’ve killed him a thousand times in my mind.”

“But…you also realized that if you were in prison—or dead—Delia and young Andrew would suffer badly.”

“Exactly!” Mario threw his hands in the air. “I don’t know what to do.”

“Our old friend Voltaire told us ‘It is forbidden to kill, therefore all murderers are punished unless they kill in large numbers and to the sound of trumpets.’”

Mario stared at Armando for a moment before breaking eye contact.

As if reading Mario’s thoughts, Armando spoke up, “I have many different interests, little cousin. Philosophy is but one of them. Give me the name of this vermin that is making your life unpleasant. Continue to make the payments until the situation is resolved. I will let you know when that has occurred.” Armando smiled pleasantly and clapped his hands together. “Now let’s try some of those pickled mushrooms you have graciously brought.”

***

It was Saturday morning. As was his habit, Fortunato Calabrese visited the kiosk Mario and Delia operated at the neighborhood vegetable market in Janesville.

Delia had taken Andrew to visit the farm this weekend, so Mario didn’t need an excuse as to why he didn’t want her at the kiosk on this particular day

"Mario! My most valuable client! How are you, my friend?"

Mario attempted to maintain a neutral tone of voice. "Good morning, Fortunato. I hope you are well."

"As a matter of fact, I am not. My physician believes our damp climate is adversely affecting my health. He recommends I spend at least one week a month in a warm dry climate, such as Las Vegas."

Mario had a suspicion as to where this was going. "Well, you certainly should heed your doctor's advice."

"My problem, good friend, is the funding of this treatment. I am just a modest agent who provides needed services to my customers. I can barely get by as it is."

Mario was coy. "How unfortunate."

"Yes, it is unfortunate. But you can help me with this dilemma, Mario, and I'm sure you will gladly do so. In the future, my services will require an extra twenty dollars per month from you...starting today."

CHAPTER 24

"**I** like the program just fine, Ray, I really do. But this security shit is driving me crazy. How long is this going to continue?" Henry Bohn complained. The U-2 flight program was shrouded in secrecy. The flight instructors, students, engineers, and technicians remained sequestered six days a week. The seventh day they were restricted to travel within thirty miles of the training facility and shadowed by Secret Service operatives.

"I don't care much for it either. My wife is threatening to move in with her parents, and the kids hardly know me anymore. But we knew this coming in. One year...one year—they told us—and the current level of security will be dropped. We'll go back to a normal life. As far as I'm concerned, with the money they're paying us, it's worth it."

Bohn frowned. "Yeah, I agreed to it. And yes, the money is fucking great. But my girlfriend dumped me the second month. The chances of me getting another date under all these damn restrictions are slim to none. I might as well have entered the priesthood."

Montrell laughed. "You'd look great in one of those tunics, Hank. And you'd get all the free wine and incense you wanted."

"They're called robes. And I don't need any stinky incense or cheap Mogen David wine."

"Okay, okay. I'll talk to management and see if we

can get 'em to loosen the leash a bit. But it's unlikely with this new development." Montrell lowered his voice and addressed a more serious matter. "Have those charts turned up?"

As with all documents and material in the program, training charts were classified as top secret. According to protocol, they were never to leave the training building. Additionally, they could not be photocopied or handled by anyone without a top-secret clearance. Three documents from Hank's class were missing.

Hank pursed his lips. "I think I know where they are, I'll have them back in the files by next week."

Ray Montrell's demeanor changed. "Next week? Hank, these are top-secret documents, not recipes from Good Housekeeping. This is a serious breach of security! If management knew about it, we'd both get canned. And probably prosecuted as well."

Bohn raised both hands. "I apologize, and I take full responsibility for this. I'll talk to the students today and give the guy a chance to put them back. It's probably just an oversight. I'll make sure those documents are back in the file within two days."

"Please see that they are."

***

When the documents didn't turn up, Montrell and Bohn had no choice but to notify Jarvis Troope, Lockheed's head of security. He called an emergency meeting with Paul Schultz, Vice President of Lockheed Human Resources. Ray and Hank were on hand.

Schultz voiced his concern. "I don't need to remind anyone here how damaging to Lockheed the compromising of the information in the missing files would be. Am I correct in saying that the charts are still missing and that one of your students has not shown up for training class since you brought this to the students' attention?"

"That is correct," Montrell confirmed. "The missing student is Charles Odenay from San Diego, California."

"Jarvis, you've brought his security clearance file," said Schultz. "Anything of interest in there?"

"Nothing out of the ordinary, until you dig a bit deeper. He's a crop duster who went on to fly for the Navy. He flew in Korea and had an impeccable record. But there is one minor blemish in his file that gives us a lead."

"And what is the nature of that blemish, Jarvis?" Schultz asked.

"Apparently Odenay got into a jam with one of the locals while stationed in San Diego. It turns out that Odenay owed this guy a pretty good chunk of money in gambling debts, and the guy called him on it. After a dust-up in a local nightclub, it came to the attention of his squadron commander. Odenay borrowed money from his fiancée to pay the guy off, at the time."

"A gambling problem," Schultz remarked.

"Very likely. I've dug around a bit and it turns out he's a regular at the horse track. And from what I gather, he's unlucky."

Schultz slammed his open palm on the table. "I want everyone looking for this guy. It's our top priority at the moment."

After the meeting, Henry questioned the students again. One of them had seen Odenay on their day off a few weeks before with Jack Sharkey, an unsavory character with inside knowledge of the aerospace industry.

"Where does this Jack Sharkey operate?" Montrell asked Henry, trying to hammer out a plan regarding their errant student.

Bohn wasn't sure. "He supposedly has ties to a criminal gang in Gary, Indiana. Not the Mafia, but some independent group of thugs. Keep in mind I'm getting this third hand."

"Can we assume Sharkey is passing the charts to the Soviets?"

"I honestly don't know, but who else who would have a reason for obtaining this stuff? Do you think it's time to get the FBI involved? Should we tell Troope about Sharkey?"

"Not just yet, Hank. There's something about this whole thing that doesn't pass the smell test. Let's do some more digging around, try to find Odenay and give him a chance to come clean."

CHAPTER 25

Ishkode Redmond checked into the rehabilitation center in St. Cloud, Minnesota. He spent the first two days in detox and was clearheaded enough to meet with a professional therapist who would be with him throughout the process of eliminating his alcohol dependency.

"This is an important first step for you, Mr. Redmond," Dr. Mitchell Turner said.

"How long will I be here?"

"That all depends on you. There's no set time limit for your recovery. Some people leave in one or two months, others are here for three months before they're comfortable enough to leave."

"You mean I can leave when I think I'm ready?"

"You're not a prisoner here, Mr. Redmond. You can leave today if you wish. But if you want to regain your family and the life you had before alcohol took over, you'd be wise to stay until you're completely recovered."

Thinking of Arnold, Ishkode asked, "Can I have visitors?"

"Certainly. After two weeks, we permit visitors once a week. If you're still in recovery after four weeks, we allow visitors twice a week."

Ishkode looked around at the intimidating surroundings. "What will I do here?"

"You'll receive counseling every day, to strengthen your ability to fight off the desire to abuse. You'll also

156

attend various workshops, to develop skills in areas such as carpentry, brick laying, and landscaping. These skills will allow you to gain employment when you leave the facility."

"Will there be powwows?"

"We have an Indian therapist on duty here. He is empowered to transport you to tribal land to attend powwows, healings, and other events you desire once every two weeks. Because of resources and program requirements, the events must not exceed one day. But he's also on call here any time you wish to discuss anything regarding your cultural needs."

Ishkode considered everything Turner told him. "When will I learn who has provided the means for me to be here?"

Dr. Turner paused. "Your benefactor wishes to remain anonymous until you have successfully completed the program. He doesn't live in the area."

"How does he know me?"

"I'm sorry, but that's all I can tell you, Ishkode. I wouldn't worry about it for now. Just take advantage of this great opportunity and get well."

***

Morning Star and young Arnold Redmond arrived at the institute for their first visit. For a week, Ishkode had been eagerly awaiting this moment.

Ishkode gently hugged his young nephew. "Hello, Little Bear."

"Hello, Uncle," Arnold quietly said. He had not seen Ishkode for several weeks and had never seen him like this. Back on the res, Uncle Ishkode rarely shaved his chin hairs, nor did he wear anything but his old torn blue jeans and flannel shirt. Now clean-shaven, with his hair neatly cut and combed, wearing a pressed jumpsuit, Ishkode presented an unfamiliar figure to his young nephew.

"How are you, my nephew? Have you been working on your studies?"

"Yes, Uncle."

"He is doing very well," Morning Star said. "He excels in reading and sports."

"What about the ways of the Ojibwa?"

Morning Star said nothing. Prior to his departure, Ishkode himself had been teaching Arnold the ways of the people. Tribal leaders consistently applied pressure to Indian Affairs to add this to the school curriculum, but it seemed to fall on deaf ears. Morning Star knew it was a sensitive issue with Ishkode and avoided the subject.

"I am teaching myself, Uncle." Arnold said proudly.

Ishkode smiled and laid his hand on Arnold's shoulder. "That is good, Arnold. When I have completed my time here, we will study together."

"When will that be?" Arnold asked.

"It will be soon, I hope. Very soon."

Before Morning Star and Arnold left, Ishkode took Morning Star aside. "Take this money. The person who pays for my treatment here also gives me spending money. I have no need for it here."

"The same person sends money to me, Ishkode. We have been able to live comfortably with his help."

"Do you know who this man is?"

"No. He sent me a letter telling me he wishes to remain anonymous until you are out of treatment and our family is together again."

Ishkode was frustrated with all the secrecy. "I don't understand why this man remains hidden, I don't like hidden faces, good or bad."

"I don't understand either, but for whatever reason this man has helped us. I will not pass judgment on his intentions. It must be important for him to withhold his identity, and I will not trouble him about it." Her voice turned hopeful. "When you are finished with this program and back home, the man has promised to reveal himself. I look forward to that day."

***

Ishkode completed another day of therapy at the clinic. Over the past several weeks, he'd attended both individual sessions as well as group sessions. In his free time, Ishkode struck up a friendship with one of the other men in the program, Hal Lundergard. Hal was another World War II veteran.

Like Ishkode, Lundergard was a rather quiet individual who kept to himself during break and when not in one of the program sessions. Finished for the day, Ishkode and Hal sat together on a bench outside near the pond and flower garden. It was a pleasant day, with a few clouds passing overhead. Now and then, a fish jumped for an insect on the surface of the water.

Ishkode broke the silence. "If I was a damn Swede with a fishing boat, we'd have us a nice fish dinner tonight."

Lundergard smiled. "If I was a damn Ojibwa, I'd have a big seine to net us some fish. Looks like chow hall meatloaf and canned beans for us again, my friend."

"That meatloaf tastes like it's made of old tires from the bus," Ishkode quipped.

"I think they pick the beans from the plastic decoration bowl by the front desk." Lundergard said.

The two lapsed into silence for a time before Lundergard spoke again. "Do you think you're ready, Ishkode?"

"I think I am. My counselor says maybe one more week. So I'll stick it out another week." Ishkode was not one to pry, but he knew Hal had been in the program for five months, long past the time when others in his position had already left. "What about you, Hal?"

Hal stared at the ground. "Oh...maybe a couple more weeks, I guess." From their past conversations and therapy discussions, Ishkode knew Hal had no one waiting for him when he got out. He didn't carry on about it, but Ishkode sensed Hal was a lonely man, unsure of his future—drunk or sober.

"Hal, I'd like to ask for your help with something."

Hal brightened, "Sure Ishkode, if there's anything I can help you with, I'll be happy to do so."

With help from the institute, Ishkode had learned to reveal his feelings. "All of the time I spent at White Earth, I was not sober. I don't know how I can handle living there, facing young Arnold, knowing I was not a good person for him to be with for so long. People think I'm some kind of war hero because I lost my leg in Saipan. But I don't feel I'm any kind of hero.... I'm scared all the time. You understand that, don't you?"

Lundergard understood that all too well. "I do. In what way can I help?"

"I would like you to come to White Earth with me. We could share a lodge together. We could help each other. You would like it, Hal. There's plenty of fishing and hunting in the area, and no one to bother you but me, Morning Star and my little nephew." Ishkode knew it would be a hard sell. "Before you say anything, think about it for a couple of days."

Hal thought over Ishkode's offer for a bit. "I'm honored you would want to share your home with me, Ishkode. But I wouldn't want to be a burden on you or your family. I'll think on it. And you do the same. It would be a big adjustment for both of us. Can I let you know in a couple of days?"

"I will wait to hear from you."

CHAPTER 26

Mario Crucianelli waited two weeks before calling his cousin Armando to let him know Fortunato Calabrese had raised his monthly protection fee.

"Mario, Mario, you shoulda let me know right away. I'm going to put a stop to this. Let me work out the details and I'll call you back."

After hanging up, Armando slammed his fist on the table. "So this fucking piece of shit is reaching deeper. I was going to take care of this little pest in a few weeks. But he's gotten too greedy, and now he's shortened his own life."

"You want I should take care of this, boss?" Mezzolini's button man asked.

"No...no, I think I need a little vacation out in the country. I'm going to take a ride up there to Bubba-land and visit Calabrese myself. My cousin has been after me for a long time to visit the family, so I'll take care of two birds with one stone, so to speak."

Being familiar with the way Mezzolini took care of "birds," the button man chuckled. "Got it, boss. Have a nice trip."

***

Mario and Delia celebrated with a dinner outing, after inking the contract to lease a storefront for their burgeoning home food business. They sipped cocktails in the bar while waiting for an available table. The restaurant was one they had wistfully teased each other about on previous occasions. While Delia felt the extravagance was unnecessary, Mario insisted they mark the occasion. A pianist entertained the crowd with soft dinner music.

Delia was not accustomed to this level of luxury. "This place is nice, really nice."

Mario agreed. "If things keep going in the right direction, we'll become regulars here."

"Goodness, Mario, we needn't throw our money around to celebrate our success."

"We work hard, Delia. We should be able to enjoy the fruits of our labor."

Delia chuckled. "Okay, but let's not spend it all before we've earned it."

"We won't, but it's good to celebrate our new start. What's left to do?"

Trained as an accountant, Delia handled most of the administrative work. "Well, we have to complete the occupancy report for the city, set up an account with the IRS— oh, and we also have to get building permits for the remodeling. Have you finished the drawings yet?"

"Damn! Sell a few jars of tomato sauce, rent a little deli, and all of a sudden we need a new building just to hold all the paperwork."

"Well, we kind of knew what we were stepping into, Mario. Once it's all done and turned in, we just have to update the paperwork on a regular basis." Delia turned serious. "I have to ask you, have you talked to your cousin yet? This business of supporting his bad debts has to stop. We're going to need every dollar we make for at least the first few years."

Mario squirmed. "Yeah, I've talked to my cousin. He promises he'll only need one more month. I told him we'd do it."

"Mario, you've been saying that for months. I'm at the end of my patience with this nonsense. It has to end now."

Mario didn't want to make a scene at the restaurant. "Okay, Del, I'll call him tomorrow."

***

Mario Crucianelli was busy getting the new store ready. He painted the walls, redid the flooring, and prepared the utilities for the new coolers which would soon be delivered to the building. He and Delia had gone back and forth as to which floor to use in their new market. Mario felt that hard wood floors would give the little shop an elegant look. He fondly remembered the smell of the wood floors from his Uncle Silvio's store when he and Dante used to deliver fruit and other goods for him. But the ever-practical Delia pointed out that linoleum was much less expensive and almost as durable, so that's what Mario installed.

As Mario sat in the back room, he chatted with a special guest who had come to visit him. The bell over the front door clattered, announcing that someone had entered the building.

"Excuse me," Mario said.

As he walked to the front, anger flushed his face. Fortunato Calabrese stood just inside the door

"Good day, Fortunato." Mario's voice chilled the room. "Good day, my favorite client. I am so happy to be a part of your new business venture. The place looks much better with the new paint and flooring. When will your grand opening take place?"

"Another two or three weeks, perhaps."

"What an exciting time for you and your family. You must be so proud."

"Yes."

"Well, I won't take up more of your valuable time. If you could just pay your monthly fee, I'll be running along."

Mario's face tightened. He opened the door and walked out, holding the door open and forcing Fortunato to turn his back to the interior of the store.

"There will be no more monthly fee, Calabrese."

Calabrese's friendly demeanor disappeared. "Do you know what you are saying to me, Crucianelli?"

Fortunato didn't realize Mario had a guest in the back room. Armando Mezzolini now walked up behind Calabrese, "I think Mario knows exactly what he is saying."

"Who dares to interrupt—" When Calabrese wheeled around his anger turned into fear. "Why, Armando! What an honor to see you in our fair city. May I ask what brings you to visit us today?"

Mezzolini glared at Calabrese with malice. "I'm here to wish my cousin well on the opening of his new business."

Calabrese looked from one man to the other and turned beet red, as he realized fully the predicament he was in.

"Why, Mario! I had no idea you were the cousin of my good friend, Armando. Had I known this, I would have given you special consideration regarding our business agreement."

Mario enjoyed watching Calabrese squirm.

"And what special consideration might that have been, Fortunato?" Mezzolini asked.

"Why, I would have lowered—no, waived—I would have waived my fees for him and his lovely wife."

"That's a good idea, Fortunato." Mezzolini's voice was icy. "It's such a good idea, I think we can take it one step further. You should consider reimbursing Mario every dollar he has given you since he's obviously been 'insured' under my protection all this time."

"Yes, uh...yes. I should do that," Calabrese stuttered.

"Excellent." Mezzolini clapped him on the back. "And I think that money should be here by tomorrow morning." Calabrese was frozen with fear. "Yes," he squeaked.

"I will have it here tomorrow morning, Mario, as my good friend suggests."

Mezzolini wasn't through. He put his arm around Calabrese's shoulders and squeezed.

"And to help them through the first difficult year or two, it would be very generous of you to offer them an interest-free loan."

"Ah. Yes...yes, I should do that...ah," Calabrese stuttered. "Please excuse me now, so I can make the arrangements."

As Calabrese rushed through the open door, Mezzolini's voice followed him. "Tomorrow morning, Calabrese."

After Calabrese's brisk exit, Mario and Armando shared a hearty laugh.

"Thank you, Armando. Thank you very much."

"It was my pleasure, cousin. I hate that little weasel. If he doesn't make good on his promise or if he gives you any more trouble, you let me know. Now, let's go see that family of yours."

CHAPTER 27

"When was the last time you saw him?" Ray asked. The problem with the stolen files had taken a turn for the worse. The prime suspect, Charles Odenay, had briefly turned up, then disappeared again.

Bohn was frustrated as well. "I saw him three days ago when I called the students together and asked about the files. After that, he called in sick and I haven't heard from him since. I went to his flat today and the landlady told me she hadn't seen him for a few days. He normally cuts her lawn as part of the rental agreement, and she was pissed off because the lawn is overgrown."

"Damn. You suppose he's skipped town altogether?" Bohn had more sinister thoughts. "Or maybe he completed the job and his partners decided it was a good time to eliminate a connection. We don't actually know how long he's been taking files. He could have been copying them and replacing them for a long time before we noticed they were missing."

"Much as I dislike Jarvis Troope, we're going to have to get him involved at this point."

"I suppose so," Bohn agreed, "but he'll come in with some 'shoulda let me handle it in the first place' bullshit. We're gonna catch more flak about this than we ever saw over Tokyo."

"You're right about that. Still no luck with Odenay's family?"

"No, his father's long dead, his mother's an alcoholic, in and out of detox. His sister's the only one who responded, and all she wanted to know was whether there was a reward involved."

"Not exactly the Ozzie and Harriet Nelson family," Montrell said.

"Not exactly."

***

Jack Sharkey delivered the final package Odenay had taken from Lockheed. After this meeting, the agreement between Sharkey and the buyer of the confidential documents would be concluded.

Carl Disheltt had been his contact with the buyer and he now accepted the final package on their behalf. "Fine job, Mr. Sharkey, may I call you Jack?"

Sharkey was gruff as always. "You may call me Mr. Sharkey."

Momentarily put off, Disheltt continued. "This delivery should contain the remaining data our organization needs. At least I hope it does."

Most people who crossed paths with Jack Sharkey knew him to be somewhat of a prickly individual. "Why the fuck wouldn't it?" Sharkey wanted to know.

Disheltt held his hands up. "No reason at all. I'm sure it does. We have every confidence in you, Mr. Sharkey. We'll meet right here again in an hour to pay you, once we've verified the information."

"Just make sure you've got the complete and final payment," Sharkey warned. He still owed a small percentage to Odenay, who'd been spooked by Bohn's questioning and phone calls. Sharkey figured Odenay was ready to bolt as soon as he got his money. He'd been hiding out in a seedy hotel for the past two days, waiting for Sharkey to collect the final payment.

Disheltt had another concern. "There is one last detail that needs to be addressed Mr. Sharkey."

"What do you mean 'one last detail'? Our business is done when you verify this file."

Disheltt pursed his lips. "Well, yes, but you see... management is uncomfortable leaving loose ends, Mr. Sharkey. Their wishes are that no middle man between you and the company the documents came from would remain...shall we say...viable."

Sharkey knew where this was going. "I'm not a goddamn hit man, Disheltt."

"What if there was a significant bonus involved?"

Sharkey thought about that.

"How significant?"

***

Jarvis Troope spent three weeks chasing down the leads from Ray and Henry, investigating both Charles Odenay and Jack Sharkey. The FBI stepped in once he found substantial evidence regarding the organization that had solicited both Odenay and Sharkey.

Troope called Montrell and Bohn to his office to fill them in, leaving the worst news for last. "An extensive search has led the FBI to Charles's body. He was stabbed in the throat and buried under mounds of garbage in a waste disposal facility outside of Toledo."

Montrell was saddened by the news. "Oh, God. No one deserves that. I'm really sorry to hear it."

"That's very unfortunate," Bohn agreed. "Odenay made some bad choices and it cost him his life. It's a real shame. When he was here he was a good student and seemed to be an all right guy. What the hell happened?"

"Must've gotten in over his head with the gambling, again," Troope speculated. "Someone was putting the squeeze on him for the money, I guess."

Montrell was in a bit of shock. "I'm still having a hard time believing this about Cranshaw Avionics. We know some of those guys."

Cranshaw was an up-and-coming defense contractor that often competed with Boeing and Lockheed for government contracts. Cranshaw, a privately held firm, had been losing out on contracts for five years and was pressed financially. Having the plans for the U-2 aircraft would have given them a step up in the bidding process.

Troope had additional information. "Turns out their board had hired Jack Sharkey before, on several occasions when they needed someone for a, shall we say, less than ethical endeavor. And now Sharkey's turned up missing as well."

"Do you suppose he's buried somewhere or maybe just gone into hiding?" Bohn wondered.

"The FBI thinks he was responsible for Odenay's demise and has gone into hiding. He has connections in Eastern Europe. They believe he will turn up there, in time."

"Will the FBI go after him?"

"Technically, it falls into the jurisdiction of the CIA if he makes it out of the country. However, since the FBI hates their guts, it's a toss-up who—or if—anyone goes after him. Have you implemented the new security procedures for the files?"

Montrell had seen to all the new security procedures. "We have, as of last Monday, no one is permitted in the file room or the classroom alone."

"Have you submitted the rest of the names for the extended background checks?"

"Taken care of," Bohn replied. "Each existing student and all future students' complete files will be submitted to the FBI contact you provided."

Troope now wanted to clear the air. "I'll be honest with you guys, when this first happened, I blamed you for it. I even thought you might have been involved. But the investigation shows that nothing you could have done under the existing conditions would have prevented the theft. And you've done an excellent job in helping us track down the perpetrators. I'm sorry for any hard feelings I may have created."

"No sweat. We would have been disappointed with anything less from a desk jockey like you." Bohn grinned. "Just kidding, Troope. We didn't do much to endear ourselves to you, either."

Montrell asked. "But what about the files?"

Troope filled them in on the complete investigation. "We've been able to recover all the files as well. Cranshaw was missing some crucial details, though, so they wouldn't have profited anyway."

"Well, it looks like this is all behind us now." Montrell extended his hand across the table. "We've got a program to run and men to train. I believe we've all learned from this experience. Let's move on."

CHAPTER 28

Ishkode Redmond successfully completed the program at the clinic in St. Cloud, Minnesota. He was now home at his lodge with his sister-in-law Morning Star and nephew Arnold. The small home had been remodeled, adding a bedroom, dining room and an updated kitchen.

Ishkode's treatment at the facility involved a series of group and individual meetings. Not one to lay his feelings bare for all, Ishkode usually remained silent in the group sessions. The individual therapy meetings started out slow as well, but Ishkode gradually opened up to the counselor. Ishkode's depression and drinking, it seemed, were a result of his belief that the loss of his leg also cost him his status as a warrior.

Counselor Jillings caught Ishkode's eye. "Who was the most important man in our nation during World War Two?"

Ishkode thought about that for a bit. "I guess President Roosevelt...maybe."

"I think so, too." Jillings replied. "A man of character, resolve, and conviction. A great leader in my opinion."

"Yes, I guess he was."

"When you think of President Roosevelt, what do you remember about him?"

Ishkode had to think about that for a minute or two. "Well, he was always in charge. He was a good leader."

"Even though he was disabled with polio and had to use a wheelchair to get around?

171

Ishkode made the connection. "Yes, I remember that now. The polio didn't stop him from doing his job."

"Ishkode, would you agree that President Roosevelt was a warrior?"

"One of the greatest warriors of them all.

"You are also still a warrior, Ishkode."

Ishkode knew at that moment there was hope...there was hope!

***

Although Hal Lundergard had not one trace of Ojibwa blood in him, he now shared the Redmond's family home. Together, the now enlarged family gathered at the ceremonial stone to honor the spirit of Chibenashi Redmond. A special guest was in attendance as well.

"I wish to express our gratitude to you for everything you have done, Mr. Heiglman." Ishkode said. "It is good to finally meet you. Please tell us how you came to know of our family."

"Just Abe, please. And you are very welcome. I'm sorry to have withheld my identity, but I felt it was for the best until you were all together again." Abe paused to collect himself. "Several years ago, I enlisted in the United States Marine Corps. As a Marine, I was sent to Korea to fight in the war there. It wasn't easy for a small Jewish kid from New York to fit in and be accepted by the U.S. Marines. Some did and some didn't. One who did accept me was Chibenashi. The only thing that mattered to him was how I performed and conducted myself as a Marine. He was one of the finest people I ever met."

Abe took a couple of deep breaths. "The citation from Chibenashi's Silver Star Medal describes his act of heroism as 'sacrificing his own life to save a fellow Marine.' Well, I was the Marine that Chibenashi saved."

"Oh, my." Morning Star put her arms around Abe and hugged him.

Abe hugged her back, then continued. "I am alive today with a wife and two children only because a great man selflessly threw himself on a hand grenade to save my life. Chibenashi is on my mind and in my heart every day. And he will be for the rest of my life."

In Chibenashi's honor, the group left a Dream Catcher, a Crucifix, and a Star of David next to the large rock before they departed.

CHAPTER 29

" Crucianelli's grand opening!" the loud speaker blared.

Mario and Delia Crucianelli bustled back and forth, serving people in their new store, Crucianelli's Deli & Liquor. The grand opening featured an accordion player, balloons and banners, and free samples of tasty Italian delicacies. Dressed in gala costumes, their two children greeted people who entered the store. Friends and family came to wish them luck, including the parish priest, Gustav Dietz, and Armando Mezzolini.

Mezzolini and Dietz sipped wine and chatted as the crowd came and went.

"So you soldiered with Mario in Korea," Mezzolini said.

Dietz laughed. "Yes, the two of us managed to get into trouble with everyone over there."

"I heard about your little escapade with the Korean prisoner. You were lucky you weren't shot."

"We almost were...by the damn North Koreans and by our own firing squad. But by the grace of God we are here. Your cousin is my best friend and a damn good man."

"Yes, he is," Mezzolini agreed, "yes, he is."

CHAPTER 30

DAYTON, OHIO

After three years of teaching, Raymond Montrell became a pilot once again, as stipulated in his contract with Lockheed. This time, he flew U-2 planes, which he'd been training others to fly since joining Lockheed. Henry Bohn was promoted to the head of the U-2 training program.

"Good luck to you, Henry. Keep these kids on the straight and narrow."

"Will do, Ray. And good luck to you as well. Keep the ground underneath you...and the commies as well. I'll keep an eye on Cora and the kids while you're up there making mischief."

"I appreciate that! I'll be back on leave every three months. I'll let you know what we're doing up there. Make sure the new guys know which way the wind is blowing before they take off, buddy."

"That's a roger, Ray. That's a roger."

EPILOGUE

"What have you learned about this Phu Cat?" Ray Montrell asked.

After high school and a short stint in college, Ray's son Doug joined the United States Air Force. Doug had hoped to become a professional baseball player, but that chance diminished after he dropped out of college. With the war in Vietnam raging, he decided to follow in his father's footsteps and enlist. Six months later he received orders to Vietnam.

"It's a large airbase in an area known as the Central Highlands of Vietnam. It's about thirty miles inland."

An astute historian and news junky, Ray was more familiar with Vietnam—both the war and the country—than his son. "And it's in the province of Binh Dinh, one of the most volatile provinces in Vietnam. The Binh Dinh province chiefs' lifespan is about three months. And they don't die of natural causes."

Doug hoped to tamp down the negative aspects of the tour. "My duty in base supply won't take me off base much, as far as I know."

"True, but the base itself is subject to frequent mortar and rocket attack by the locals. From what I've read, they aren't too thrilled with our presence over there."

"No duty is entirely safe, Dad. But my duty will be much safer than Army and Marine grunts that are humping out in the bush day and night. And you didn't have it too safe in World War II or Korea, for that matter."

"It's just that your father has doubts about the legitimacy and eventual outcome of this war." Doug's mother added her concerns. "We don't want to lose you over a war that we don't entirely believe in."

"Would you rather I run off to Canada and shirk my duty? Now honestly, you wouldn't want me to do that would you? A lot of my friends are in Vietnam right now. Some have come and gone already."

Ray Montrell was torn. "No, I wouldn't want to see that, Doug. But like your mother said, I don't want you to come to harm over a big damn mistake."

"I know how you feel about the war, Dad. I certainly don't completely understand it either. But if good Americans are over there doing their duty, well...that's where I belong as well."

As Doug's mother sniffled a bit, Doug's father beamed. He could barely speak. "We're proud of you, son. We'll always be proud of you. And we will be here for you when you return."

***

LATE 1969

SOUTHEASTERN WISCONSIN

Andrew disappeared into the Greyhound bus. Delia, Mario, and Gus gave a last wave, although they couldn't see him.

As Delia sniffled into her hanky, Mario attempted to assure his distraught wife. "He'll be okay, Delia."

Andrew would take the "Grey Dog" to Mitchell Field in Milwaukee to catch his flight to San Francisco, where he would report to Hamilton Air Field for two weeks of advanced small arms training. After his two weeks were up, Andrew Crucianelli would board a Flying Tigers chartered DC-8 for the long flight to Vietnam. In Vietnam, he'd take several more flights to reach his final destination at the Phu Cat Airbase in Binh Dinh Province in the Central Highlands.

"Who will watch over him?" Delia's voice quivered.

"He's in the military now. They're a band of brothers. They watch over each other," Mario said.

"They didn't take care of Dante." Delia noted, recalling Mario's older brother who'd been killed in World War II.

Mario tried to sound hopeful. "Delia, you just have to remain positive. Andrew's tour in Vietnam is one year. He'll be back with us for our next Thanksgiving dinner."

"A year is a very long time to wait for your child to come home from war."

"The year will go by quickly, Delia." Gus Dietz had accompanied the Crucianelli's today. As Mario's wartime buddy, family friend, and godfather to Andrew, Gus felt it was important to support the family on this momentous occasion. "You must keep your mind off of it." He added.

"How? Tell me how I'm supposed to do that, Gustav— to not worry that my son will be killed or hurt in this crazy war that I don't even understand."

Dietz had reservations about the war as well. As far as he was concerned, the United States got suckered into it by the French, who couldn't hold onto their colonial possession without assistance from the superpower.

"All wars are crazy, Delia, I've been in two of them, and neither one made sense to me. But from everything I've learned, humans have always waged war on each other. You can run off and hide, you can stay home and try to stop it...or you can go fight it. Andrew has done the honorable thing. Like you, I will pray for Andrew every day. When he comes home—and he will come home—Mario and I will take him on the best damn fishing trip he's ever had."

Delia hugged the big German and sobbed. "Thank you, Gustav. I love you dearly."

Mario threw his arm around Dietz's shoulder as well. "Thank you, Gus, I'll look forward to that fishing trip. Very much."

***

LATE 1969

WHITE EARTH INDIAN RESERVATION

Morning Star Redmond spoke to her only son. "You have honored the spirit of Chibenashi and also the spirit of Ishkode, Arnold. They would be proud of you. I am proud of you."

"Thank you, Mother."

Arnold Redmond—son of Chibenashi, killed in action in Korea, and nephew of Ishkode, wounded in action in World War II and since deceased—was home on leave after receiving orders for duty in Vietnam.

Arnold had joined the Air Force after a short stint in the Marine Corps—a stint that ended with his discharge as a result of a brawl initiated by another Marine who had insulted his ancestry.

"As much as I hate to admit it," the Air Force recruiter told him, "there are ignorant people in all branches of the service. You will either have to control your reaction to them or remain a civilian. The choice is yours, Arnold," Master Sergeant Wally Barnes said. "I can't guarantee you won't be subjected to the same type of harassment."

Arnold had learned that lesson the hard way and was determined to gut it out. All of his ancestors were warriors, and he was committed to continuing that tradition. He had breezed through Air Force basic training, aced technical school, and was on his way to Phu Cat Airbase, Republic of Vietnam.

Arnold and his mother Morning Star continued the spiritual ceremony in honor of his late father and uncle. They placed a dream catcher over the special stone they often visited. The large boulder, buried in the earth not far from their village, represented the enduring spirit of ancestors who had passed before them.

Although Morning Star was proud of her son, she was also in distress. "This war is like the lake during a storm. Many forces are at play and things are unclear. You must protect yourself, Arnold."

Arnold rubbed the surface of the large boulder. He remembered how as a boy he loved the smooth feel of the big rock. His mother had told him the spirit of the stone traveled with all the tribal warriors.

"Tribal elders will look after you until I return, Mother."

"But who will look after you, my son?"

"The spirit of the stone, Mother. And the spirits of my father and my uncle."

The story continues…

EXCERPT FROM THE KANSAS NCO

"We got some new men comin' in," reported Master Sergeant Charles Prentice, noncommissioned officer in charge of the supply and storage detail at Phu Cat Air Force Base, Republic of Vietnam.

"FANGS, huh? Well, we could use some new guys, Charley," Doug Montrell said. He and Terry Hardy were working in the back of the steamy tool-issue center, sorting tools. Perspiration was running off their bodies like water off a duck. The tool center had been short of men for months, and the tools—scattered all over the warehouse—were in total disarray.

Prentice gave Montrell a sharp look. "New men, Monty, and don't you two fuck-offs give 'em a hard time and run 'em outta here. We need to get this place up to snuff or it's your ass and my ass, so when they get here, you show 'em the ropes and treat 'em right."

"Okay, Charley, take it easy. We'll take care of the newbies when they get here, don't worry about it. When you gonna get the Kansas NCO to let us in on a gig?"

At the mention of the Kansas NCO Prentice looked around the dismal warehouse as if someone might overhear them. "Don't you worry about him, Montrell. You got enough trouble keepin' me and the first shirt happy. Besides, you know Richards don't let hippies work for him.

182

If he needs anyone to show him how to drip acid, he'll call you two goldbricks."

Montrell and Hardy roared with laughter. "It's drop acid, Charley... Drop acid!"

Prentice was exasperated. "Well, whatever the hell it is, he don't want any!"

**

"Hurry up and wait, hurry up and wait," Flash complained. "What the fuck we supposed to do, hang around here till our DEROS date?" Unfortunately for Flash and Cru their date of estimated return from overseas was thirteen months away.

"What the fuck you new meats still hangin' around here for?" A buck sergeant walked into the tent wearing dirty jungle fatigue with STANGL on the name tag.

"We were waiting for someone to tell us where to report, Sergeant," Andrew Crucianelli informed him.

"Well, get your ass to the supply warehouse on the double and make sure you have your orders with you," Stangl barked.

Flash, never one to take bullshit from anyone, barked back. "We supposed to have ESP or something, Stangl? You wanna tell us where the supply warehouse is, or do we have to find out right from the Old Man?"

"Don't get smart with me, new meat. I'll have your ass out on the perimeter for your first month in-country," Stangl responded angrily.

At that Flash stood up to his full height, intimidating the much smaller Stangl into retreating back to the opening of the tent.

Crucianelli stepped in between the two, not wanting trouble from day one. "We will report to the supply warehouse with our orders, Sergeant Stangl we just need directions."

"Take the road we're on and go right. Follow it around

to the flight line and keep your eye open for a large metal warehouse. It's got a sign on it that says BASE SUPPLY." With that he quickly left.

At the supply warehouse Flash and Cru met Sergeant Prentice. "Where're your duffel bags?"

Looking at each other, Cru and Flash explained they left them at the tent where they bunked.

Prentice frowned, "Damn, we better go get 'em quick if you have anything of value in them."

Cru and Flash started out the door to retrieve their possessions.

"Hang on, we'll take the jeep," Prentice called.

After returning to the warehouse with their gear intact, the men met Arnold Redmond, who was sitting on his duffel bag outside the entrance of the building. "Damn, we got three of you," Prentice was smiling. "Follow me."

"FANGS!" the three men in the warehouse yelled. Shirtless and soaked in sweat, they came over to meet the new personnel.

"I gotta go meet with Sergeant Richards, make sure these guys are quartered and see they understand the work details they will be assigned to. I'll check in on you in a couple of days." Prentice, happy to delegate the responsibility, left.

Happy for the interruption from the hot laborious work, Montrell and Hardy welcomed the three new men. After introductions they showed them around the warehouse and explained the duty they could expect.

"We work here ten to twelve hours a day, six days a week. We usually get Sunday off, but if there's a backup of men waiting for tools, we may have to work Sunday, also. We have to pull perimeter guard every four to five weeks. That can be brutal, because it's an all-nighter and we still have to pull our day shift in this dump.

"We get a break every two to three weeks on convoy duty. We move material from here to Qui Nhon or Phu Bai or some other shithole out in the boonies. We drive either a pick-up truck or a deuce-and-a-half, depending on the load. Besides the driver and the shotgun, there are usually one or two more men in the back with the load. We can hit a whorehouse if we're lucky, and once we even got to swim in the ocean while we waited for a load in Qui Nhon.

"But it can be dangerous, we've been attacked a couple of times since I've been pulling the duty. It's usually voluntary so if you don't want to take the chance, you don't have to. You guys got any questions?"

"You guys get hit here much?" Crucianelli asked.

"The first three months I was here we didn't get hit once, except for a sapper attack," Hardy said. "Since they've been pulling the 173rd Airborne back, we've been getting hit more regularly, usually around once or twice a week. We've only had five guys killed, but there's been dozens of injuries and a lot of damage as well. It's scary and keeps us from sleeping too well."

"What are they hitting you with?" asked Arnold Redmond.

"Usually its Chi Com mortars," said Montrell. "Maybe only five or ten. Sometimes they throw in some rockets. The mortars are bad, but the rockets scare the fuck out of everyone, even the goddamn dogs."

"Where can I get screwed?" asked Flash.

Hardy laughed. "You're gonna get screwed every day you're here, buddy."

***

The Kansas NCO and its sequel *Back to the World* can be found on Amazon, Barnes & Noble, and many other online book sellers. Copies can also be purchased directly from author Joe Campolo Jr. through his website at www. namwarstory.com

ABOUT THE AUTHOR

J oe Campolo Jr. is an award-winning author, poet, and public speaker. He is a Vietnam War veteran and a veteran's advocate. He is a feature writer for Dispatches, the national quarterly magazine of Military Writer's Society of America (MWSA). Many of his short stories are published there and in other magazines as well.

Joe is an avid fisherman, and some humorous fishing stories can also be found on his blog. Joe is married and has two children, two grandchildren, and lives in the state of Wisconsin.

Joe may be contacted through his website at www. namwarstory.com